B·I·B·L·E LEGENDS

An Introduction to Midrash

VOLUME TWO : EXODUS

LILLIAN FREEHOF

With introductions and commentaries by
HOWARD SCHWARTZ

Illustrated by PHYLLIS TARLOW

UAHC Press ◆ New York, New York

Talmudic references throughout this book are from
the *Talmud Bavli,* the Babylonian Talmud.

Library of Congress Cataloging-in-Publication Data

(Revised for vol. 2)

Freehof, Lillian S. (Lillian Simon), 1906–
  Bible legends.

  Bibliography: v. 1, p.143–145; v. 2, p.
  Contents: v. 1. Genesis — v. 2. Exodus.
  Summary: A collection of Jewish legends focusing on such primary
characters of the book of Genesis as Adam and Eve, Noah, Abraham and
Rebecca, Jacob, and Joseph.
  1. Legends, Jewish.   2. Bible stories, English—
O.T. Genesis.   3. Bible stories, English—O.T. Exodus.   4. Midrash—
Juvenile literature. [1. Folklore, Jewish. 2. Bible stories—O.T.
Genesis.   3. Midrash]
I. Schwartz, Howard, 1945–   . II. Tarlow, Phyllis, ill.   III. Title.

BM530.F73   1987   296.1′4205   [398.2]   87–13799
ISBN 0–8074–0357–1 (pbk. : v. 1)
ISBN 0–8074–0412–8 (pbk. : v. 2)

Publication of this book was made possible
by a generous grant from the

AUDRE AND BERNARD RAPOPORT
Library Fund

Contents

Introduction

By general agreement the two most important figures in the Bible are Abraham and Moses: Abraham because he was the first Jew, the first to have the intuition that there is only one God; Moses because he freed the Israelites from Egyptian bondage, received the Torah on Mount Sinai, and led the people to the Promised Land. Without either of these towering figures, Judaism as we know it would not exist.

The central roles played by Abraham and Moses endeared them to the rabbis, who referred to Abraham as *Avraham Avinu,* "our father Abraham," and Moses as *Mosheh Rabbenu,* "our teacher Moses." The rabbis, of course, spent a great deal of time studying the Torah and meditating on every aspect of it. As a result, they grew curious about those events in the lives of the patriarchs not related in the Torah. For example, nothing is written in the Torah about the childhood of Abraham, although legends existed about his childhood in the oral traditions of Judaism. These legends described the events of Abraham's youth in terms almost identical to those of the child Moses: how the evil ruler Nimrod (instead of Pharaoh) was told by soothsayers that a Hebrew child would overthrow him, resulting in the command to slay all firstborn Hebrew male infants; how Abraham's mother went off to a remote cave to have her child, to prevent its slaying if it was male (while Moses' mother hid her baby boy in a little ark, left floating on the Nile). In both cases a miraculous event takes place: the infant Moses, floating on the river, is found by Pharaoh's daughter, who adopts him and raises him as an Egyptian prince; the infant Abraham is sustained and protected by the angel Gabriel sent by God. The baby sucks the angel's thumb from which milk and honey flow. From this miraculous food the infant grows a year a day; in less than two weeks he grows to Bar Mitzvah age, educated by the angel in speech, the ways of the Torah, and many other mysteries.

How is it possible that the traditions concerning the childhoods of Abraham and Moses could be so similar? To understand this, it is first necessary to know something about the Oral Law. According to traditional Judaism, as long as the Jews have had the Torah (the Written Law) they have had a second tradition known as the Oral Law. One rabbinic legend relates that God dictated the Torah to Moses on Mount Sinai during the day and explained it at night. These explanations are said to make up the Oral Law.

From the first it was understood that the legends and other traditions of the Oral Law would not be written down, but they would be passed on by word of mouth from one generation to the next. For more than a thousand years, these oral traditions were indeed transmitted this way. After the destruction of the Second Temple in Jerusalem, however, it was considered necessary to transcribe them, lest they otherwise be lost. The text that resulted from writing down the Oral Law is known as the Talmud; still more of these legends were later collected in texts known as the Midrash.

When we speak about a midrash, we are referring to either a rabbinic legend from the Talmud (an *aggadah*) or a legend from the hundreds of volumes of midrashim. All these texts are regarded as sacred by the Jews because they are said to contain the vast traditions of the Oral Law.

The very vastness of this oral tradition, however, raises another question: Were all these legends really passed on by Moses from Mount Sinai? No one can answer this for certain, but it seems likely that, while some of the legends of the Talmud and Midrash are indeed very ancient, others were created by the rabbis themselves, as a way of explaining problems in the biblical text or such gaps in the narrative as the missing childhood of Abraham. Utilizing what we might call the midrashic method, the rabbis supplied missing details from hints found in other passages of the Bible.

Still the question remains: Did the rabbis themselves believe that all the legends of the Talmud and the Midrash came from Moses at Mount Sinai? It is hard to reply with certainty, but one legend in the Talmud (*Menachot* 29b) seems to hint at the answer. The Bible describes how Moses ascended Mount Sinai to receive the Torah, but the Talmud says that, once he reached the top of the mountain, he ascended all the way into Paradise. There the angels, who had not been enthusiastic about the creation of human beings in the first place and did not want Israel to receive the precious Torah, tried to frighten and intimidate Moses, who finally was forced to call out for God's help. God commanded the angels to let Moses pass safely. When, at last, Moses reached God's throne, he saw that God was weaving something. "What is it that you are weaving?" asked Moses. "I am weaving the crowns of the letters of the Torah," God replied, "so that in the future a man named Akiba ben Joseph will be able to interpret every crown and letter of it." "Master of the universe, I would like to see him," said Moses. "Turn around," God answered. And, when Moses turned around, he found himself sitting in the back of the classroom of Rabbi Akiba—who would not be born for well over a thousand years! Rabbi Akiba was explaining a point of the Law to his students, a point that Moses, although he tried his best, found he could not understand. At last one of the students raised his hands and asked Rabbi Akiba: "From where do we learn this?" And Rabbi Akiba answered: "From Moses at Mount Sinai."

What, then, does this legend tell us? It seems to hint that the rabbis knew that some of the traditions that had evolved in Judaism were not part of the original heritage of Mount Sinai and that even Moses would be surprised by them. And, in telling this tale, the rabbis are acknowledging a very important point: Judaism must change and evolve in order to adapt to the times in which it is practiced. When we consider that Jewish tradition reaches back three thousand years and is still a flourishing religion, we can recognize that this is truly a miracle in itself, and we should not be surprised if the way it is practiced today differs from practice during the time of Moses.

Among the great contributions of Moses, none exceeded the receiving of the Torah. Of course, the term "Torah" has come to mean more than just the Five Books of Moses. It also symbolizes all of Jewish law and legend, for in the broadest sense this is all an extension of Torah.

It is not surprising, then, that there are a great many legends about the Torah itself in the Midrash. One of the legends tells how the Torah was created before the creation of the world and was held in waiting until the time came to reveal it to Moses on Mount Sinai. Another legend tells how the Torah was secretly revealed to such key figures before Moses as Adam, Enoch, Noah, and the patriarchs, Abraham, Isaac, and Jacob. This legend builds on the first, presuming that the Torah already existed before it was given to Moses and the children of Israel. And it resolves a difficult problem for the rabbis: how the Torah, the central text of Judaism, could not have been known by the patriarchs.

Furthermore, the Midrash tells us that the giving of the Torah took place over the objections of the angels. When Moses ascended into heaven to receive the Torah, he had a spirited debate with the angels, in which he pointed out to them that the Torah was intended for humankind and not for them, to which the angels agreed in the end.

Still another legend observes that Moses had to receive the

Torah twice. The first time, as he descended from Mount Sinai with the Tablets of the Law in his arms, he saw the people worshiping the Golden Calf, and in his great anger he smashed the tablets. Therefore, he had to reascend the mountain in order to receive them again. This legend speculates that the Ten Commandments engraved on the first stone tablets were different from those on the second tablets. Indeed, this midrash suggests that the original Ten Commandments were all positive, "You shall . . . ," rather than negative, "You shall not. . . ." Since the people had shown that they could not be entrusted with the positive commandments, it became necessary to state some of them in the negative. Thus this legend suggests that the breaking of the first tablets was a major event in human history, not unlike the Fall of Adam and Eve, which resulted in their expulsion from the Garden of Eden. This same midrash goes on to speculate that the letters on the first stone tablets were written in fire and that, when Moses smashed the stone tablets, the letters flew back up to heaven.

All of these legends demonstrate the midrashic method of trying to read between the lines of the Torah to discover the hidden meanings and missing portions ("midrash" comes from the word *drash,* "to search" or "to discover"). These legends reveal a great deal about the thinking of the rabbis and demonstrate clearly how deeply they cared for the Torah, seeking solace and understanding in its every word. Thus these legends give us considerable insight into the minds of the sages whose teachings helped shape and enrich Judaism.

It is appropriate, then, that the rabbinic legends collected in this second volume of *Bible Legends: An Introduction to Midrash* largely concern Moses because of his deep involvement in every aspect of the great epic of the Exodus from Egyptian bondage, the receiving of the Torah, and the wandering in the wilderness in search of the Holy Land. Mrs. Freehof, drawing upon the legends of the Talmud and Midrash and upon the scholarship of Louis Ginzberg, author of the monumental *The Legends of the Jews,* has retold these legends vividly, remaining true to her sources.

In these stories we learn, for example, about the magical staff of Moses, which turned into a serpent in Pharaoh's court and later was used by Moses to part the waters of the Red Sea and to bring forth water from a rock, and about his combat with the giant Og, king of Bashan, who without God's help might have single-handedly destroyed all Israel. We find out details about such a miracle of the Exodus as the manna that fell from heaven to feed the people. We learn also the details of the mysterious death of Moses, of which little is said in the Torah.

Each of these stories makes considerable use of the midrashic method to explain, embellish, and enhance the biblical text. To learn additional details about these legends and their backgrounds, read the commentaries that follow each story. You are also encouraged to try to write your own midrashim, using the time-honored methods of the rabbis.

Howard Schwartz

❦ 1 ❦

The Gold Crown and
the Live Coal

The childhood of Moses contains many elements characteristic of the childhoods of other mythical or legendary heroes. The prophecy that a Hebrew male child would one day overthrow Pharaoh led to the decree that all Hebrew boy babies be slain at birth. The infant Moses escaped this fate when the little basket in which his mother had put him was discovered by Pharaoh's daughter as she was bathing in the Nile. So it was that Moses was raised in the palace as if he were royalty, giving birth to the legend in which the baby Moses arouses Pharaoh's fears— fears that would eventually turn out to be well-founded.

Malol, the pharoah of Egypt, sat with his court at dinner. On his head rested his glorious crown, heavy and golden.

This crown was tall and broad, hammered out of gold, with sharp little points on its top. A big emerald was set squarely in its center. Around the emerald were stones of every shape and color, diamonds and rubies, pearls and sapphires. Pharaoh was proud of this crown, and he guarded it jealously. He permitted no one to touch it but himself. The courtier who helped him dress could not brush even his little finger against it because Pharaoh, the mightiest one in the kingdom, had one fear. He

1

was afraid that, if anyone dared so much as to *touch* his crown, that person would snatch from his control his kingdom and his power.

On this particular evening, Pharaoh and his court sat in the banquet hall of his palace. Linen cloths were spread on the tables, set with gold plates and gleaming goblets for wine.

He sat in the center of this long and heavily laden table, his glorious crown settled firmly on his head. Next to him, on his right, sat his queen, Alfaranit. At his left sat his daughter, Princess Bithiah. And on her lap sat the little boy Moses, whom she had adopted as her son.

All around them sat the princes of Egypt, the nobles, and the wise men. Servants scurried about, carrying platters loaded with all kinds of delicious foods. The wine stewards rushed around filling the wine goblets, never permitting them to remain empty. And so Pharaoh and his court, without a care in the world, were eating heavily, drinking merrily, and enjoying themselves.

The child Moses, too young to eat at the king's table, had already had supper. It was past his bedtime, but his mother, Bithiah, wanted the boy with her a little longer. So she sat him on her lap, and everyone in the court was amused at the sight of the little tot at the royal table.

Moses was a clever child, but he couldn't talk very much as yet. While everyone else was eating, he amused himself by picking up whatever his pudgy fingers could reach. He played with his mother's gold spoon. Then, tiring of the spoon, he dropped it on the floor. His little hand clutched at a piece of food on Bithiah's plate, and she said, "No, no, mustn't touch." His other hand reached out and touched the gold braid on the sleeve of Pharaoh's robe, but his hand was so tiny and had so little strength that the king didn't feel him pulling.

Moses put up his hand and touched the king's face, and Pharaoh turned and smiled at him. Moses clapped his hands, squealing with delight. And the king went on with his feasting.

Then Moses put his two hands on the table, pushed himself up, and stood on his mother's lap. Bithiah said, "Moses, dear, please sit down."

Moses remained standing. Suddenly, before anyone guessed what was happening, his two small hands darted out, pulled the crown off Pharaoh's head, and set it on his own!

Great excitement! So great was the hubbub that for a moment there was just a loud shouting of voices. Then, over the confusion, Pharaoh yelled, "My crown! Who took my crown?"

Everybody shivered. Moses smiled.

Pharaoh turned and saw his magnificent gold crown perched on the child's head. Moses was clapping his hands, laughing for joy.

"Montrous!" Pharaoh shouted.

"That wicked child!" cried Queen Alfaranit.

"Naughty, naughy," Bithiah scolded, not really angry because she thought what Moses had done was very cute.

But she was the only one who thought so. Everyone else was shocked and angry and terrified at what Pharaoh would do. First, he roared. Then he snatched the crown from Moses' head and clapped it back on his own. Twice he pushed at it to make sure it was on securely.

A hush fell on the assemblage. Pharaoh pointed his finger at one of his princes.

"Balaam," Pharaoh ordered, "behold this infant. Take him. Behead him!"

The people gasped at the king's command. But Princess Bithiah's voice rose above the loud cries.

"Oh, no, Father," she cried. "No, no. Little Moses meant no harm. He is just a baby. See, he doesn't even realize what he did."

Everyone, even Pharaoh, looked at little Moses, and one or two people giggled nervously. The baby was gurgling and cooing, trying to fit a napkin on his head.

"See," Bithiah pleaded, "now he's trying to make a hat of

the napkin. He's just a baby, Father. He didn't understand."

"Well." The king began to soften. His voice dropped from a shout, and the red began to leave his face. "He committed a crime, a serious crime. No person in the world is allowed to touch my crown!"

"But he's only a baby. . . ." Bithiah began again, but her father silenced her with a gesture of his hand.

He motioned to the nobles and the princes to gather around him. They came quickly. He rose and said majestically, "You saw this dire deed. You know this baby is a Hebrew child. Do you think he took my crown with a purpose? Or do you think it was an innocent act? I will give you two minutes to consider this matter. Then I want your opinions."

Queen Alfaranit spoke up. "I always said no good would come of Bithiah's adopting that Hebrew child."

Pharaoh did not answer her. Instead he turned to Bithiah and said, "Take the child to your palace. We shall discuss and decide his fate."

Bithiah rose and walked out of the banquet hall, holding Moses tightly in her arms. As she walked through the long, stone corridors, her footsteps echoing in the stillness, she thought back to the day she had found Moses.

The story had had its beginning three years earlier. Pharaoh had had a dream in which he saw an old man holding a pair of scales. Into one scale the old man put all the princes and nobles of Egypt; into the other scale he put a little lamb. And behold—the scale with the lamb weighed more than the scale with the great men of Egypt! The king was troubled by this dream, and he asked Balaam, the son of Beor, to explain it.

Balaam said, "The scales are the symbol of your kingdom and your throne, O Pharaoh. The little lamb stands for a Hebrew child. Your dream means that one day there will be born a little Hebrew boy who will destroy you, your kingdom, and all of Egypt. Therefore, O Pharaoh, to safeguard your kingdom, you must destroy every Hebrew male child at birth."

This was cruel advice, but the king followed it. He issued a command that all the boy babies of the Hebrews be slain the moment they were born. But, when Moses was born, his mother hid him in a little boat. She made a little ark out of bulrushes, put him in it, and set it to float on the river.

That same day, Princess Bithiah had gone with her ladies-in-waiting to the Nile River to bathe. When she saw the little ark, she rescued it before it could float out to sea. She opened it and saw the tiny baby, and she was delighted! Having no children of her own, she took Moses and raised him as her son.

She was remembering all these things now as she sat in her own palace, waiting for her father to summon her to the banquet hall. She watched Moses at play in his golden crib, wondering what her father and his wise men were deciding.

Back in Pharaoh's banquet hall, the wise men were talking.

"He's just an innocent babe, as Bithiah says." Ruel, the Midianite, spoke first.

"No, he's a grasping child," Job, the Uzite, said. "He shows signs of great selfishness."

"No, no," said Balaam. "Listen to me. It is worse than selfishness. It means danger to Pharaoh. This Moses, O Pharaoh, is a very dangerous child. You remember your dream of the lamb who weighed heavy in the scale of your kingdom? I warned you then that one day some Hebrew child would destroy you and your kingdom."

"Yes, yes," the king said anxiously, frightened again. "Too well do I remember it!"

"This child Moses is that lamb of your dreams, the child who will crush you and Egypt," Balaam warned.

"Nonsense," Ruel said. "Princess Bithiah's child did not know what he was doing when he placed Pharaoh's crown on his own head."

"I don't agree with you," Balaam said angrily. "He is a Hebrew child. The Hebrews are smart people. Because he is a Hebrew,

Moses knew very well what he was doing. O Pharaoh, I suggest—nay, I *urge*—that you slay this child."

Ruel held up his hand. "One moment, please! This punishment is too severe for this crime. Why be so cruel? Your Majesty, may I suggest that you call together all the wise men of Egypt? Put this problem before them. See if they agree that this child shall be slain."

Pharaoh approved this suggestion and issued a call for all the wise men of Egypt to come immediately to his palace.

Up in heaven, God and the archangels listened to this argument in Pharaoh's palace. Now God said, "Gabriel!"

Gabriel stepped forward.

"Gabriel," God commanded, "go down to earth. Disguise yourself as one of the wise men of Egypt. Mingle with them and protect Moses."

Gabriel listened, smiled, and bowed low. Then swiftly he flew away from heaven.

When all the wise men were gathered in Pharaoh's palace, Gabriel was among them. No one dreamed he was an angel. His disguise was perfect. He listened with the others while Pharaoh explained what had happened. When Pharaoh finished, Gabriel spoke up quickly before anyone else could even catch his breath.

"O Pharaoh," Gabriel said, "this is a very serious matter, and I know you are anxious to discover the truth. Is Moses a cunning child who wickedly snatched your crown or is he an innocent babe attracted by a beautiful object? If you put Moses to death, you will never know the truth. Let us put little Moses to the test."

"What an absurd idea!" Balaam interrupted. "How can you test a child?"

Gabriel answered quietly. "Of course you can test a child. I will tell you how. Bring the child here. Place before him an onyx stone and a coal of fire. The fiery coal is bright but worthless. The onyx stone is dull but is a precious jewel. If he is cunning, he will put his hand out to the precious gem. If he is innocent, he will grasp the worthless coal. If he takes the onyx stone, we shall know that he is clever and guilty. Then slay him."

"Good, very good," Job agreed.

"But," said Gabriel, "if the child grasps the burning coal of fire, then we shall know that he is a foolish child, that taking your crown was just innocent play. And he shall live!"

Pharaoh nodded, and all the wise men were quick to agree, exclaiming, "Splendid! A splendid plan!"

Pharaoh sent one servant to fetch Bithiah and the child, another servant to the treasury to bring the onyx stone, and a third servant to the kitchen to carry in the coal of fire. All came immediately.

The stone and the coal were placed on the table before Moses. Everyone stood watching breathlessly. Bithiah's heart was beating fast because she was afraid that the clever child Moses would pick up the precious stone.

For a moment Moses made no move toward either. He was clapping his hands and laughing at all the funny faces in front of him. There were so many people to see, he didn't know where to look first. But Balaam was getting impatient. He said to the child, "See? Pretty things? Pretty?"

Moses reached out his hand. Everyone watched breathlessly. Which would he take?

He reached his fingers towards . . . the onyx stone! But the angel Gabriel, quickly making himself invisible, thrust Moses' little hand away from the stone toward the coal. And Moses picked up the hot coal! And, as a child does, he put it to his mouth, and started to cry. His cry was drowned in the cheers of the people.

"He is innocent!" they yelled. "Moses shall live!"

And so his life was saved. He was allowed to live; but forever afterward he spoke with a lisp because, when he put the burning coal to his mouth, it burned his tongue.

Commentary

When she opened it [the basket], *she saw that it was a child, a boy crying.*   Exodus 2:6

*   *   *

After the story of Abraham and the idols, perhaps the best known midrash is the story of how the infant Moses snatches Pharaoh's crown. Taken as an ill omen by Pharaoh and his soothsayers, they contrive a test of the infant's intentions, holding out the crown in one hand and a glowing hot coal in the other. The child is drawn to the crown, but the angel Gabriel pushes the hand of Moses to take the coal, which he naturally brings to his mouth, burning his tongue. Thus the story offers an explanation of why Moses stuttered. (*Sefer Hayashar*) This is a fine example of how the Midrash embellishes a story, providing explanations for unaccounted facts, such as the speech defect of Moses, while at the same time foretelling Moses' later victory over Pharaoh.

*   *   *

In the story of the child found in a basket by an Egyptian princess and raised as royalty, we find the outline of a fairy tale. Moses' staff is magical, turning into a serpent in Pharaoh's court and later causing water to spring forth from a rock. If we look closely, we find many fairy tale elements in the Bible: the two enchanted trees in the center of the Garden of Eden and the speaking serpent, the whale that swallows Jonah, and the talking ass in the tale of Baalam. Perhaps the one book of the Bible that most resembles a fairy tale—with a king, a queen, an evil vizier, and a wise old man—is the Book of Esther.

*   *   *

Pharaoh's dream in which a small lamb outweighs all the princes and nobles of Egypt was interpreted by the court sooth-

sayers as a prophecy that Pharaoh would be defeated by a Hebrew. According to the Midrash, this led to Pharaoh's decree
(Exod. 1:22) that all male Hebrew infants be slain. This is not
the reason given in the Torah, where the Egyptians are said to
fear the rapid increase in the number of the Israelites. Note
the parallelism between Pharaoh's dream at the time of Moses
and the prophetic dream of Pharaoh at the time of Joseph. In
both cases the dreams use an animal to symbolize the competing
forces of the future: cows to symbolize plenty and famine in
one case, and a lamb to symbolize the Jews in the other. Linking
the two Pharaohs in this manner also has the effect of linking
Joseph and Moses. The Midrash often makes such generational
connections.

Write Your Own Midrash

It is known that Moses was raised in Pharaoh's palace as the
child of Pharaoh's daughter, the princess. However, except for
the legend just related, nothing is known of the life of Moses
before, as a grown man, he killed an Egyptian overseer. Imagine
what the life of Moses was like in Pharaoh's palace. How did
he learn his true identity? How did he view his Jewish brethren
who were serving as slaves? In the palace, was he treated as
the son of the princess or as an adopted Jewish child? Did he
try to learn more about the God and religion of the Israelites?
Were there any incidents in which his true identity was revealed
to him?

≥ 2 ≥

The Devouring Tree

After killing the Egyptian overseer whom he found beating two Hebrews, Moses had to flee Egypt. Little of his ten-year absence is recounted in the Torah, and thus it became a fertile subject for the legends of the rabbis. Between the time that he had to flee and the period in which he encountered the Burning Bush, the primary event recorded in the life of Moses was his marriage to Zipporah. From the midrashic perspective, an equally important event was Moses' discovery of his rod (or staff), to which the rabbis attributed a glorious history. In the Midrash these two events are woven together.

Moses, on his way home to Egypt from Ethiopia, reached the city of Midian. It was early in the morning, and as he came to the well he noticed a great commotion. A mob of people milled around the well. They were shepherds who had come to draw water for their flocks.

They rushed around, talking loudly. Some were laughing. Some were calling to one another. Others were bending over the well, shouting down into it.

As Moses came close, a man on the edge of the group saw him.

"Halt, stranger," he said angrily. "What are you doing here?"

Moses answered quietly, "I come from Ethiopia and on my way back to Egypt my journeys brought me here to Midian. But tell me, what is the excitement at the well?"

"Oh, that?" The man laughed loudly. "Just a little fun we're having. You see, stranger, here in Midian lives a man whose name is Jethro. He has seven daughters. They must do the work of the shepherds because we will not work for their father."

"Why not?" Moses asked.

"Because," one man said angrily, "he's gotten some peculiar notions into his silly head. He says he believes in only one God!"

"Imagine," sneered the first man, "he worships a God you cannot even see!"

"And today, stranger," another man said, "today we threw all seven girls into the well!" The man broke into a fit of laughter.

"Thrown into the well!" Moses began to push through the crowd. "They will drown! Make way, make way, before they drown."

"Let them!" cried one man roughly. "They worship an unseen God."

"I too worship the unseen God!" Moses said sternly. "Throw me into the well if you dare!"

The men began to mutter angrily, then, looking at Moses standing proudly, his tall strong body straight, they were afraid. They began to push backwards against each other, pushing to get away, still muttering, still pushing. Then, suddenly, they turned and ran.

Moses forgot them because he was busy pulling the girls out of the well, all seven of them. It took quite a time because it is no easy matter to pull up seven girls. As each one, soaking wet, was set safely on the ground, she threw her arms around the sisters already rescued, and, as if they were not wet enough, they all began to cry.

Moses reached the seventh girl. This one did not weep. Her eyes blazed with anger. She looked as mussed up as her sisters, her wet dress clinging to her body, her long hair, dripping water, plastered to her head. But that head she held high. She gazed directly at Moses and said, "My father is Jethro. My name is Zipporah. I thank you, sir, for rescuing my sisters and me."

She turned to the girls and told them to fill their buckets and get along home. Then she invited Moses to come to their home to have breakfast and to meet their father who would want to thank him, too.

The other sisters, chattering excitedly, hurried on ahead. Moses and Zipporah walked more slowly and talked. He told her who he was and where he was going, and she told him how she and her sisters had to tend their father's sheep. As they walked and talked, Moses liked her more and more. And finally, just before they reached her home, he said, "Zipporah, I have searched everywhere for a girl like you, all over the East, in Egypt, in Ethiopia, and nowhere did I find her till I came to Midian. Now I have found you, I want to marry you."

"That you can never do," Zipporah answered sadly. "The tree will not let you marry me."

"The tree?" Moses exclaimed. "You mean a tree growing in a garden? How can a tree stop me from marrying you?"

"The tree will devour you."

Moses laughed. "I have never heard of a tree that eats people. You are joking."

"Oh, no," she answered. "In my father's garden there grows a magic tree. If you tell my father you wish to marry me, he will ask you first to pull that tree out of the ground. You will try. But the moment you touch that tree, it will devour you. I have seen it happen. Every young man who has tried to marry me or my six sisters has been devoured by that tree."

"Where did your father get this magic tree?" Moses asked.

"It's a long story," Zipporah said. "But I will tell you. When God first created the world, at twilight of the first Sabbath eve, God created a rod. It was the Sapphire Rod. God gave this rod to Adam. Adam gave it to Enoch, Enoch to Noah; then it descended from Noah to Shem, to Abraham, to Isaac, and then to Jacob. When Jacob went to Egypt he gave it to Joseph. Upon Joseph's death, it came into Pharaoh's possession. At that time my father was a scribe in Pharaoh's court. From the moment my father saw the Sapphire Rod, he longed to own it. When he came here to Midian to live, he took it from Pharaoh and brought it here. One day my father was walking in his garden. He stuck the rod into the ground. When he tried to pull it out, he couldn't! It had rooted itself into the ground and sprouted! It became a tree!"

"I must ask your father to tell me more!" Moses said, interested.

"Oh, no!" Zipporah begged, "please do not let him know that I have told you the history of the tree."

"Very well. When I ask to marry you, he will tell me about it himself."

They reached Zipporah's house. She brought him in and introduced him to her father who had already heard from the other girls the story of the rescue from the well. He greeted Moses and thanked him for saving his daughters. Then he sent the girls to change into dry clothes. They went, giggling, chattering about their adventure and this handsome man from Egypt.

Moses told Jethro who he was and how he came to be traveling about. Then they talked of Ethiopia and Egypt.

Zipporah had changed out of her dripping wet dress into a lovely, flowing pink gown, trying to get back to Moses and her father as quickly as she could. But, as she entered the room where the two men sat talking, her sisters came running after her. As she approached, Moses smiled at her. Then he said, "Jethro, I want to marry your daughter, Zipporah."

Jethro smiled.

"You seem to be a fine young man," he said, "a man to make a good husband for my daughter. But, before I can give my consent, there is one thing I must ask you to do."

"Ask," Moses answered. "I will gladly do whatever you ask."

Jethro smiled again. "In my garden there is a small tree. All I ask is that you pull this tree out of the ground."

"Certainly," Moses agreed. "That can't be too hard."

And all the girls shivered.

He smiled confidently at Zipporah, then stood aside to let Jethro precede them into the garden. All the girls followed their father. Zipporah came last. As she passed Moses, she whispered, "Are you sure you will try? At the risk of your life?"

Moses smiled and nodded and followed her out to the garden.

He looked at the tree. It was just like any ordinary tree. It had a trunk and branches and leaves. Then suddenly, before his eyes, the tree seemed to change. Now the trunk looked like pitch and the branches like coils of rope and the leaves like steel-jawed traps! This tree ate human beings! It devoured anyone who touched it! And Moses was afraid.

Moses closed his eyes, the better to remember that he had been brought up as a prince, had already helped the suffering Israelites in Egypt, and had conquered the country of Ethiopia. He knew that any man who had done all these things could not be devoured by a mere tree. A tree growing in a garden could not hurt him. With these thoughts he conquered his fear.

He opened his eyes. Once more the Devouring Tree looked just like any other tree. Behind him Zipporah and her sisters stood holding their breath. Moses touched the tree.

The leaves curled around his fingers! The branches stretched out like arms and hugged him to the rough bark of the trunk. Then, as he felt himself being drawn into the tree, he whispered, "Tree, Tree, I know you are no tree. You are the Sapphire Rod which God gave to Adam, which Adam gave to Enoch, to Noah, to Shem, to Abraham, to Isaac, to Jacob, and to Joseph. O Sapphire Tree, I am a descendant of Joseph, of Jacob, of Isaac, and of all those back to Adam. I am a child of God."

The branches loosed their hold. "O Sapphire Tree, do not devour me. Do not hurt me." The leaves uncurled from his fingers.

Zipporah's sisters whispered excitedly, but she said nothing. She just stood watching.

Now Moses grasped the tree in both his hands, leaned forward, strained his muscles—and pulled—and pulled—and suddenly, with a shower of loose dirt, out from the ground came the tree, roots and all! And in his hand the branches withdrew into the trunk, the trunk grew slim, and the tree became again the Sapphire Rod.

Quietly, without a word, Moses handed the rod to Jethro.

"The tree did not eat him!" the sisters cried together.

"The tree is gone!" one of them cried.

"Moses is safe!" cried another.

And then they all wept and laughed. They danced and sang. Because now someday they too could be married. Moses had destroyed the Devouring Tree and Moses was their hero!

Because he had brought joy to all of them, the sisters made his wedding to Zipporah the most wonderful wedding ever held in Midian.

Commentary

And take with you this rod, with which you shall perform the signs.   Exodus 4:17

*   *   *

Sometimes the Bible contains elements similar to those we find in folk and fairy tales. One such element is the rod (or staff) of Moses, which he uses to perform several miracles. With it Moses makes the waters of the Red Sea part. (Exod. 14:21) Later, in the wilderness, he uses it to strike a rock from which water then pours forth. (Num. 20:11) The staff of Aaron also displays miraculous properties, turning into a snake in Pharaoh's court. When Pharaoh's sorcerers duplicate this trick, the snake of Aaron devours those of the sorcerers, demonstrating its superiority.

(Exod. 7:10–12) In each of these cases, the staff works in much the same way as a magic wand works in fairy tales, except that in Jewish lore it is well understood that the source of the staff's power comes from God, not from magic. Naturally the staff of Moses was a prime subject for the Midrash, which traces the history of the staff and provides a miraculous story explaining how Moses obtained it.

* * *

It seems that the rabbis' favorite legends were those linking several generations of patriarchs and sages. These legends are known as chain midrashim. (See "The Blue Sapphire Book" and its accompanying commentary in *Bible Legends: An Introduction to Midrash,* Volume One: Genesis.) To those who regard the stories in the Bible as a series of unrelated events, the rabbis would offer these special midrashim that serve to link all of Jewish history into a continuous chain. A classic example of the chain midrash concerns the staff of Moses. As Moses learns in "The Devouring Tree," the staff has a fantastic history. It was one of the objects created at the time of the creation of the world and given to Adam. It then belonged to Enoch, Noah, and the patriarchs before ending up in the garden of Jethro, where none but Moses could pull it from the ground. Note that this legend links Moses to Adam, Enoch, Noah, Abraham, Isaac, Jacob, and Joseph. It makes the role of Moses in that distinguished line indisputable, and it gives continuity to Jewish history.

* * *

Most Jewish legends are derived from Jewish sources. That is, the rabbis turned primarily to other passages in the Bible when they sought to embellish one passage that they felt needed further explanation. A good example of this is the midrashic story of Abraham's childhood, which is precisely modeled after that of Moses. (See "The Wonderful Child" and "The Garden in the Fire" with accompanying commentaries in the first volume of *Bible Legends: An Introduction to Midrash*.) However, on occasion a Jewish legend is based on a non-Jewish source. The most common sources were Greek, Christian, and Moslem legends. Not that the Jews sought to imitate the legends of a neighboring people, but it is simply the nature of folklore to be shared. Thus it is also possible to find extensive Jewish elements in both Christian and Moslem lore.

In the case of the legend of the staff of Moses, however, we have an example of a Jewish legend based on a Christian source—and a famous one at that. One of the most famous Christian legend cycles concerns King Arthur, and the key legend tells how Arthur pulled the enchanted sword from a stone, thus demonstrating that he was destined to be king. Essentially the same legend is found in the Midrash—though in a late source, dating from at least the twelfth century—and tells how Moses pulled the enchanted staff from the garden of Jethro. There are, in fact, two basic versions of this legend. One (*Sefer Hazichronot* by Jerahmeel ben Solomon, compiled by Elazar ben Asher Halevi) is almost identical to the Arthurian legend; the other ("Wa-Yosha" 42 in *Bet Hamidrash* by Adolf Jellinek), on which the story in this book is based, adds the new element of the devouring tree. That is, the staff not only resists the efforts of those who try to pull it out when they are not destined to, but it has taken root and blossomed and devours those who make the unfortunate attempt to uproot it. (See "The Rod of Almonds," chapter 9 of this volume, and its commentary concerning the theme of a staff that blossoms.)

This reworking of the Arthurian legend resolves several problems: it gets the staff into the hands of Moses; it shows that Moses belongs in the distinguished line of those who had previously possessed the staff; it makes it possible for Moses to marry Jethro's daughter, Zipporah; and finally it identifies him, in a sense, as "king" of the Jews—what we would more appropriately call a prophet—who would free his people from bondage, receive the Torah, and lead them to the Promised Land. From this we learn something of the way a folk tradition works: it draws upon whatever is at hand, no matter what the original sources, transforming it into something unique to its own tradition.

Write Your Own Midrash

What happened to the staff of Moses? Jewish legend does not trace its history after Moses. Therefore it is an ideal subject about which to write a midrash. Perhaps you can invent a story of how King David found the staff and how he made use of it. He, in turn, could give it to his son, King Solomon. You may want to create the history of what happened to the staff after the destruction of the Temple. Perhaps it could be found by some key figure such as the Baal Shem Tov, founder of Hasidism, or it could even be found by a modern day hero like David Ben-Gurion, the first prime minister of Israel. There are many possibilities. One of the pleasures of writing your own midrash is choosing the one that most appeals to you.

⚜3⚜

Let My People Go

Moses was a reluctant prophet, shy by nature and afflicted with a severe speech defect, the origin of which is given in the tale, "The Gold Crown and the Live Coal." Yet Moses, well aware of his true background, identified with the Hebrew slaves of Egypt. His sympathy for them led him to strike and kill one particularly brutal Egyptian overseer, forcing Moses into exile. During this difficult period Moses encountered the Burning Bush and heard the voice of God. Thereafter his life was transformed as he reluctantly accepted his destiny to free the Hebrew people. This turned out to be no simple matter, for Pharaoh was not about to free so valuable a resource as his slaves. Thus the stage was set for a monumental confrontation.

All over Egypt trumpets were sounding. This day was Pharaoh's birthday, and everyone was celebrating. Soldiers marched. People sang in the streets. Young girls danced.

The palace was surrounded by an army. There were four hundred entrances to the palace, and at each entrance sixty thousand soldiers stood guard. To these entrances came all the princes of the land and the rulers of the neighboring countries, bringing gifts to Pharaoh. Each person who entered the palace carried a crown for the king.

Moses and Aaron, too, came to the palace, but they were not celebrating Pharaoh's birthday. They came to one of the entrances, but they were not bringing a crown for the king. Aaron carried a staff; otherwise their hands were empty.

As they approached one of the south entrances, the soldiers would have challenged them because they were not carrying a gift for the king. But Moses and Aaron stood tall and straight, holding their heads high, their appearance dignified and regal. So magnificent were they, so impressive, that the guards dared not challenge them. Instead they whispered to each other, "These must be great nobles from some far kingdom. Stand aside, there, stand aside."

The guards saluted and formed an aisle through which Moses and Aaron walked slowly and in stately manner through the entrance, into the court, up to the presence of the king. They bowed their heads in greeting, and Pharaoh said to them, "Welcome. It is kind of you to come to do me honor."

Then he saw that they carried no crown to present to him, no gift to give him. Puzzled, he said, "What is your gift for me? Where is the crown you would offer me? Who are you?"

Moses answered quietly. "We are Moses and Aaron. We bring you no gifts. O Pharaoh, you hold in your hand the life and liberty of six hundred thousand Hebrews. Permit the Hebrews to leave this land. Let us be free to go into the wilderness. There we will worship our God."

Pharaoh laughed. When the nobles and visiting rulers saw that he was amused, they laughed too, and soon the whole palace was filled with laughter so loud that it drowned out the blare of the birthday trumpets. Moses and Aaron stood quietly by until Pharaoh, weak from laughing, had to stop. He looked at the two men waiting patiently.

"What!" he exclaimed, "are you still here? For your impudence, I would behead you. But you have amused me, so I shall let you live. Asking me to free six hundred thousand slaves! Impudence! Now go, go. I am no longer amused. You begin to irritate me. I am busy. I have many nobles to receive and many presents to accept. I have no time to waste with you."

"O Pharaoh," Moses said, "the God of the Hebrews bids me say to you, 'Let My people go!' "

Pharaoh was no longer laughing. Now he was impatient. "What foolishness is this? On my birthday everyone brings me gifts. They add to my wealth. But you come and ask me to give up six hundred thousand slaves! You want to rob me and make me poor. Indeed, you are fools or crazy. Go now from my presence."

" 'Let My people go,' " Moses repeated. "Thus says the God of Israel."

"The God of Israel. I have never heard of this God." Pharaoh looked around at those present, and they all shook their heads. "I don't know of any such God." He turned to one of the courtiers. "Fetch me the book of chronicles from the royal library. I shall see whether the name of this God of the Hebrews is in it."

The book was brought to him. He looked into it. And he read, "Here are the names of the gods of Moab, the gods of Ammon, the gods of Zidon. Oh, I thought so! Nowhere in this book do I find the name of the Hebrew God." He turned angrily to Moses. "You deceived me. You invented this God to cheat me out of my slaves."

Moses stood proudly, lifting his head high. "God's name is not in your book of gods. Your gods are dead, written on the walls of your tombs and pyramids. Our God is the living God. The names of the idols you find in your book are only idols, false gods; but our God is the God of life, who rules forever."

"How this impudent man raves in my royal presence!" Pharaoh shouted, at the end of his patience. "Who is your God? What are your God's powers and strengths? How many countries are under this God's control? How many cities and provinces does this God rule? How many battles did your God win? How many countries did this God conquer? When your God goes into battle, how many soldiers, riders, chariots and charioteers does this God lead forth?"

"I speak to you without fear," Moses answered. "You think of our God as you think of a human being. Listen now to me, O Pharaoh.

"God's strength and power fill every corner of the earth. The heaven is God's throne, and the earth is God's footstool. God's bow is fire, God's arrows flames, God's shields clouds, and God's sword the flash of lightning. It was God who made the mountains and the valleys. It was God who made man and woman and the souls within them. With a single word God created the whole of the earth. Over the heavens God stretched the clouds, and when God pronounces the word the dew and rain fall to the ground. God is the Might and the Power and the Glory of all the world!"

"Stop!" Pharaoh commanded. "Enough! Put an end to this silly prattle. I do not know your God. Your God has no claim on me. Why should I obey the commands of an unknown God?"

"All God asks of you, O King," Moses said, "is that you permit the Hebrews to leave this land."

"Your request is absurd," Pharaoh grumbled. "How can you expect me to grant it? If perhaps you had asked for a thousand people, I might do so, I am a gracious ruler. . . . Yes, what do you say, just to end this argument, if I give you one thousand of your people?"

"No." Moses stood firm. "All the people must go."

Pharaoh turned to his wise men. "You see how unreasonable this man is? I would let a thousand go, but no, he demands six hundred thousand slaves! Come now, come, let us have no more of this. I am weary of it. Go. Get out of my sight."

The royal bodyguard moved towards Moses and Aaron to speed them on their way. But neither Moses nor Aaron moved one step.

Moses spoke. "If you do not let the Israelites depart from

here, O Pharaoh, our God will bring trouble to this land, sending plagues of every kind."

Pharaoh laughed. "You cannot frighten me. There is nothing your God can do that would harm me."

He turned away to join in the merrymaking of his court, and Moses and Aaron stood to one side. Servants came running, bringing bowls of grapes and dishes of cherries, and Pharaoh and his court ate heartily. The trumpets were sounding, the musicians strummed their instruments, dancing girls swayed to the rhythm of the music. Everywhere in the palace there was laughter and joy and merrymaking.

Suddenly the king clapped his hands. A servant came bowing and scraping. Pharaoh said, "Bring me a bowl of water that I may wash my hands. The grapes have made my fingers sticky."

The servant brought a bowl of water to the king and other servants brought basins to the nobles and the visiting rulers, but, when they dipped their hands into the water, at the touch of their fingers, the water turned into blood! They all shrieked, flinging the blood away from them.

At the same time a courtier came running in, crying, "All the wells have turned to blood. The Nile River has turned to blood."

Pharaoh turned angrily to Moses. "Is this a trick of your God?"

"This is one of the plagues I warned you about. Let the Hebrews go, and the water will turn pure again."

"Throw these men out!" Pharaoh yelled, and two guards came forward. They pushed Moses and Aaron at the point of their spears until the two were outside of the palace walls.

There they waited, knowing they would soon return and plead again.

Inside the court, Pharaoh called his magicians together, told them to work their magic, to turn the blood back into water. Each sorcerer tried every magic trick he knew, but without success. Meanwhile, the people became thirstier and thirstier, their throats parched, their tongues swollen. And Pharaoh began to get uneasy. Afraid of a revolt, he sent for Moses and Aaron.

When once more they stood before Pharaoh, Moses said, "I say to you, 'Let my people go.'"

Pharaoh said quickly, "Turn the blood back into water, and I will let your people go."

Moses and Aaron went off into a corner and whispered a prayer and, in a twinkling, the blood turned into water. When Pharaoh saw the clear, sparkling water in the bowl before him, he and the people drank and drank and drank.

Then Moses said, "Now I shall take the people of Israel and go."

"No!" shouted Pharaoh. "Did you think I was serious when I promised that? Nonsense! I just wanted the water to be pure again."

As he said the last word, without warning, in an instant, the whole floor of the palace swarmed with frogs—big frogs, fat frogs, green frogs, squeaking frogs, croaking frogs, smooth frogs, warty frogs. They darted. They scurried. They leaped onto Pharaoh's throne, up the legs of the dancing girls, into the musicians' instruments. Every chair, every table, every person was covered with frogs.

At that moment a courtier came running in, shouting, "Frogs are everywhere! Frogs are overrunning the land!"

Pharaoh was stunned. The people were frightened. Moses and Aaron stood quietly to one side. There were no frogs crawling on them. Pharaoh beckoned to Moses, who came and stood before him.

"Is this another trick of your God?" he shouted.

"There is worse to come," Moses said quietly, "unless you let my people go."

"I promise!" Pharaoh cried, brushing frogs from his shoulders and from his knees. "I promise. Tell your God to make these frogs vanish. I will let the Israelites go!"

When Moses and Aaron had whispered their prayer, as suddenly as the frogs came, so did they disappear. Everybody sank back into their chairs, weary and sick from fighting the frogs.

"Are they really gone?" Pharaoh asked, opening his eyes.

"Ugh." He shivered. "It was dreadful. I never want to go through anything like that again."

Moses walked to the throne. "Now that this plague is withdrawn, I must remind you of your promise. Let the people of Israel go."

"What!" Pharaoh laughed. "You foolish one. I never meant to keep that promise."

Moses, in a rage, called upon God to bring the next plague to Egypt.

And so it went. With each plague Pharaoh promised to release the people. The moment the plague was removed, he broke his promise.

God sent the plague of the locusts and the plague of wild beasts, the plague which destroyed the food and the plague of serious illnesses. Terrible plagues, horrible plagues God sent, and each time Pharaoh promised, and each time he broke his promise.

Then Moses went once more to see Pharaoh.

"O Pharaoh," he said, "how stubborn you are. How hard is your heart. I come to you for the last time. I shall give you my last warning. If within one hour you do not let the Hebrews leave Egypt, then God will kill the firstborn in all the land, the firstborn child of every family, the firstborn of all the cattle. Release the children of Israel. Let them go, or the firstborn of Egypt will die within the hour."

Moses and Aaron did not wait for an answer. They turned on their heels and left the palace. Fifteen minutes passed. A half-hour went by. Three-quarters of an hour speeded away. Still Pharaoh sent no message. The hour came—and went.

One minute after the hour, a great wailing arose over all of Egypt. The firstborn cattle and the firstborn children, young or old, fell dead. And the people went shouting to Pharaoh.

"Let the Israelites go or we shall all be dead," they yelled.

They threatened to revolt. And now Pharaoh was really frightened.

He called a guard to him. "Go. Find Moses. Tell him to come before me."

The guard delivered the message, but Moses shook his head. "I no longer believe anything Pharaoh has to say. I warned him that I had come to him for the last time. If he wishes to see me, he will have to come to me."

When Pharaoh heard this answer to his summons, he wanted to stamp his foot and yell at the top of his voice and order Moses beheaded. But he was too frightened to be angry. He, the high and mighty, he, the great king, Pharaoh—*he* went to see Moses. A company of soldiers marched with him. At the door of Moses' house, he knocked.

Moses called out, "Who is there?"

"It is Pharaoh. Open up to me, Moses."

"Pharaoh?" asked Moses. "Is it true that the king himself has come to me, Moses, an ordinary human being?"

"I beg of you, Moses, most honored Moses," Pharaoh pleaded, "please come forth out of your house. Raise your voice and plead with your God to stop this plague or there will be no one left alive in all Egypt."

Moses remained silent, and Pharaoh pleaded again, in a loud voice. "Please, Moses, if you will not come forth out of your house, then I beg of you, come to the window and speak with me."

Moses went to the window and spoke before Pharaoh could say another word.

"This time, O Pharaoh, you will not have a chance to break your promise. This time, before I ask God to end this plague, you yourself will release the Israelites."

"I promise!" Pharaoh cried. "I promise!"

"Then, Pharaoh," Moses said, "raise your voice and shout aloud, 'Children of Israel, you are your own masters. You are free to leave Egypt. You have been my slaves up to now. Now you are free to serve your God.'"

Pharaoh raised his voice and shouted, "Children of Israel,

you are your own masters. You are free to leave Egypt. You who have been my slaves are now free to serve your God."

"Shout it aloud twice more," Moses commanded.

And twice more Pharaoh shouted the words in a thundering voice that could be heard all over the land.

Within the hour, six hundred thousand Israelites began to march out of Egypt. They struck off their iron chains. They broke their shackles. They lifted their heads high. They marched out of Egypt as a free people.

And God ended the last plague, for the children of Israel were free.

Commentary

Thus says the Lord, the God of Israel: Let My people go.
Exodus 5:1

*   *   *

The saga of the Exodus from Egypt, a central episode of Jewish history, is recreated each year at the Passover Seder. As we read from the Haggadah, the biblical account of the Exodus is relived, and each participant is required to say, "We were slaves to Pharaoh in Egypt," suggesting that our understanding would be enhanced if we imagined ourselves living through the experiences of our ancestors. Another rabbinic tradition holds that, just as each of us was a slave in Egypt, so too was every Jewish soul present at the giving of the Torah at Mount Sinai. In such ways did the rabbis demonstrate their personal involvement in Jewish legend and history, which in turn transformed their daily lives.

Write Your Own Midrash

Since the Haggadah encourages us to imagine that we were slaves in Egypt, write a midrash from the point of view of one of the Israelites wandering in the wilderness with Moses for forty years. It could be someone named in the Bible, such as Aaron or Miriam, or it could be one of the anonymous people who made the long journey. Describe, from an individual perspective, events such as the falling of the manna, the revolt of Korah, the creation of the Golden Calf, or the giving of the Torah.

✹4✹

The March through the Sea

After the tenth plague, which killed all the firstborn in the land of Egypt except those of the Hebrews, Pharaoh finally relented and let the Hebrew people go. But soon afterward he regretted this decision, and his advisers convinced him to chase after and retrieve the slaves. So it was that the Israelites found themselves trapped at the Sea of Reeds (often called the Red Sea), with the chariots of Pharaoh rapidly approaching from behind. It was at this moment that the greatest miracle in Jewish history took place.

Moses and Aaron rode together at the head of the ranks. Everything had gone according to schedule, yet Moses was uneasy, and he whispered his worries to his brother.

"It hardly seems real, Aaron. Are we really leaving Egypt? Is Pharaoh actually keeping his word? Somehow, someway, I feel that all is not well. Why did Pharaoh let us go so easily?"

"So easily?" Aaron asked in astonishment. "Think back over the plagues! Have you forgotten? It was only after a long struggle that he let us go. Oh, no, I don't think he let us go easily!"

"No, Aaron, there is something wrong. After each plague Pharaoh broke his promise. Why is he letting us go this time?

I don't know, Aaron. Something is wrong. I feel uneasy."

Moses was right to worry.

Back in his palace, Pharaoh sat slumped on his throne, with his courtiers at attention in front of him, everyone silent, everyone gloomy. The Hebrews were gone. They had lost six hundred thousand slaves. How would they now build their cities? Who would do their back-breaking work?

"What a fool I was!" Pharaoh said aloud, suddenly. "Why did I let the Israelites go? Why did I do such a foolish thing?"

"What will we do for slaves?" Balaam asked.

"Who will do our work for us?" asked his son Jambres.

"Who will build our storehouses?" asked Jannes.

"Who, indeed?" Pharaoh muttered. "I was wrong to let them go. Attention! We shall go in pursuit of them! We will bring them back! Those who will not return will be put to death. Ready the chariots! Gather the armies! Forward!"

Everyone jumped up and began to rush about wildly. Pharaoh, excited at the thought of capturing the Israelites, did not wait for a courtier to harness the royal chariot but did it himself, with his own hands. Others worked at top speed, and in one hour hundreds of chariots were racing through Egypt, with Pharaoh at their head, and behind them thousands of horses carrying warriors, and behind them ran thousands of foot soldiers. A mighty host pursued the Israelites.

Because they rode in swift chariots and had three drivers to each instead of two, they speeded over the ground faster than the fleeing Israelites. In one day they covered the ground the Israelites had traveled wearily in three days.

Moses had called a halt at Pi-hahiroth, and, while they were resting, their sentries saw the Egyptians coming from afar. They ran to Moses and told him the dreadful news. The Egyptians were coming!

The people were stricken with fear! And with good reason. On both sides of them were the wild beasts of the desert. If they went through the desert, the wild animals would devour them. Behind them came the charging Egyptians. Before them was the Red Sea. If they tried to go through the waters they would surely drown! There was no way to escape! They faced death and destruction. And in their fear they thought up wild schemes.

"We are going to die anyhow," said one group. "There is no escape. Then let us drown in the sea. It is a clean death."

"No," said a second group, "let us return to Egypt. Life is better than death, and in Egypt, while we shall be slaves again, at least we will be alive."

"Never!" shouted a third group. "Never will we return to slavery! No, we will fight the Egyptians. In battle we can redeem our honor. If we die, we die, but let us die fighting!"

"Maybe we can get rid of the enemy without fighting," said a fourth group, timidly. "Let us make a big noise, a mighty noise, and perhaps we can frighten the enemy away."

"Quiet!" Moses had to shout to be heard over all the excitement. "Quiet! We shall not drown, return to Egypt, or fight the enemy. We shall not die, but live! Have faith in God to save us. Pray! Lift your voices in prayer."

The people obeyed, and Moses himself prayed but God called down to him, and said, "Moses, why do you stand there praying? Prayer is good, but there is a proper time for it. Now is the time for action. Take the staff that you hold in your hand and divide the sea with it. Say to the sea, 'O you waters, listen to my voice. I am the messenger sent by God who created all the world! Uncover your paths, O Sea, for God's children, that they may go through your midst on dry ground.'"

Before Moses could answer, suddenly at his side appeared the archangel Gabriel.

"Quickly, Moses," he said. "Speak as God has told you."

Moses held out the staff over the sea and cried out, "O you waters, listen to my voice. I am the messenger sent by God who created all the world! Uncover your paths, O Sea, for God's children, that they may go through your midst on dry ground."

To Moses' surprise, the sea talked back to him! "Moses, I hear your words. But why should I obey you? I am older than you. I was created on the third day. Human beings had to wait till the sixth day to be created."

Moses held up the rod again, and again he said to the sea, "I repeat the divine command. Open up your waters, O Sea. It is not what I, a mere mortal, wish, but what God commands."

The sea said, "But you ask me to divide myself in two parts! To cut myself in two! Why, that will hurt me! It will give me terrible pain and agony. I'm sorry, Moses. I'd like to oblige you because you would not ask such a favor unless it were necessary. But, I'm sorry. I just can't do such a thing to myself."

The sea tossed a few waves about sullenly.

Moses in despair turned to Gabriel. "What shall I do now, Gabriel?"

"Ask God to help you."

Moses called again to God. "O God, the sea refuses to divide for me. Please ask the sea to do it. It will not refuse You."

But God answered, "No, Moses, I cannot ask the sea to divide, for, if I did, it would never again draw together and would remain divided till the end of time. But I will send down to you a little bit of My strength to help you."

Moses waited a moment until the little bit of God's strength came to his side. The moment the sea saw the strength of God at the right hand of Moses, the sea trembled and pleaded with the earth, "O Earth, quickly, make a hollow place for me. I must hide!"

Moses said, "Why are you terrified, O sea? Why? When I asked you to divide, you refused. Why are you so terrified now?"

"I am fleeing before the God of Creation," said the sea.

And as it spoke, there was a great rushing of wind, a great roaring of waters. Every drop moaned, every wave groaned, and slowly, slowly the great sea began to separate. It spread apart into two huge, high columns of water that reached towards the clouds, leaving twelve separate paths, one for each tribe of Israelites, and forming a vault above their heads.

Moses urged the people to hurry, to rush through the two banks of water on the dry land, before the sea should have to close its arms again. If that happened, anyone who was still moving across would be trapped and drowned. So the people ran and crowded and rushed onto the sand to go through and across as fast as possible. As each tribe went into its path, the people noticed that the wall of water was transparent, as glass is, and they could see their friends hurrying through the other paths.

In each pathway a small stream of fresh water flowed, so that, when thirsty, they could snatch a drink of fresh water. Then, too, no matter what a person wanted while hurrying through the Red Sea, it was there for the taking. If one wanted a red apple, one only had to pick it from the glassy wall; if one wanted a bunch of green grapes, one had only to pluck it from above.

These things were so surprising, so wonderful, that the people began to stand around in awe. It began to seem like a picnic to them, a great holiday, instead of an escape from the Egyptians. So Moses and Aaron and Gabriel had to keep rushing up the pathways calling to the people, "Hurry, hurry, move right along, please. Do not stop, please. Hurry, hurry!"

Then suddenly, the word came, like lightning, from the back ranks to the very front rows. The Egyptians were at the edge of the sea! At any moment they would ride through on the sand in their chariots and overtake them!

Moses shouted to the people, "Hurry, hurry! If you are not out of the sea in the space of ten long breaths, you will perish. The sea must close up and cover the Egyptians. If you do not hurry, you will drown with them!"

The archangel Gabriel saw that there were thousands of people still in the pathways and knew that in another moment they would be doomed. He put out his huge angel hand and, with one big swing, swept them all forward, in a great heap, out of the sea.

Without a moment to spare! As the last Israelite was pulled

off the sands of the sea, with a great sighing of every wave of its waters, with a great moaning of every drop in the floods, the mighty sea closed back on itself, drowning Pharaoh's army.

And the children of Israel, safe on the opposite shore, rescued by God and Gabriel and Moses, lifted up their voices and sang their song of thanksgiving: "In Your love You have led the people You have saved."

Commentary

The waters were split, and the Israelites went into the sea on dry ground, the waters forming a wall for them on their right and on their left. Exodus 14:21–22

* * *

Legends of the Israelites' crossing of the Sea of Reeds have great appeal, for that experience unified the Israelites as nothing else had before or after, except the giving of the Torah at Mount Sinai. The miraculous crossing spawned some wonderful legends. When the people sang in unison, for example, it was said that even the unborn children sang out from their mothers' wombs. Another legend describes how the towering walls of the parted waters were laden with delicious treats. If a mother were hungry, she simply had to reach out and pluck a pomegranate.

* * *

In another memorable legend about the crossing, the sea is reluctant to part itself, fearing that it would never again become whole. This is especially interesting because the sea, being the largest object on earth, is often viewed as a symbol for God. Thus the sea's resistance reflects the fundamental Jewish belief of the indivisibility of God.

Write Your Own Midrash

Write a midrash about the crossing of the Sea of Reeds. Describe the walls of water: Was there only one path or many? Did the people rush forward or were they afraid to cross? How close behind were Pharaoh's chariots? What was the mood of the people? What would the Egyptian troops have done to the escaping Israelites if they had caught them? The Midrash describes this crossing in great detail, noting that all the angels watched the event. What might the angels have said to one another as they witnessed the crossing? Write a midrash from the perspective of one of the Israelites.

✹5✹

Bread of the Angels

God's miracles, which saved the Israelites at the Red Sea, followed the Israelites through the wilderness. So desolate was the terrain that the starving Israelites became restless, and some ruthless adversaries of Moses—most notably a man named Korah—sought to exploit the situation. God's confidence in Moses remained unshaken, and repeatedly God intervened with miracles, demonstrating to the people that Moses was acting in God's name. The most memorable of these miracles was the appearance of manna, a divine food the Israelites found on the ground each morning that not only sustained them but tasted delicious.

L et me tell you a secret," Abiram said. "I don't like Moses."

"Neither do I," Dathan grumbled. "But the people do."

"And why not?" muttered Abiram. "Look what he has done for them already. He freed them from Pharaoh. When they were trapped by the Red Sea, he divided the water, and they passed through unharmed."

"But he had God to help him!" protested Dathan. "We're just as smart as Moses."

"And magicians besides," Abiram said. "We could be the lead-

ers. I'll make a confession to you, Dathan. I want to be the leader of the people of Israel!"

"Not a chance," grumbled Dathan, "with everything going so well for Moses."

"Yes, but just you wait." Abiram brightened up. He chuckled. "Now his real troubles will begin. Now that we're in the desert, the people will thirst and starve, and they will curse Moses and come to us for help. You'll see!"

After the miraculous escape from the Red Sea, Moses permitted the people to rest for a short while. Then he gave orders for the camp to be broken and the march forward to begin. As soon as Dathan and Abiram heard the orders, they began spreading rumors among the people.

"Do you know where Moses is leading us?" whispered Abiram.

"He is taking us to the desert of Shur!" Dathan hissed.

"What's wrong with the desert of Shur?" someone asked.

"Oh, it's a horrible place," Dathan exclaimed. "It's a wilderness, full of snakes and lizards and scorpions."

"For hundreds of miles!" Abiram rolled his eyes in pretended fear. "Nothing but scorpions and lizards and snakes for hundreds of miles!"

"These snakes are so deadly," Dathan added, "that if a bird is flying in the air, and if its shadow falls on the ground, *if* one of these snakes just crawls over the bird's *shadow,* that bird falls from the sky, dead!"

Some of the people were frightened and wanted to turn back immediately. But others were certain that Dathan and Abiram were just trying to frighten them. Moses, they said, would not have gone to all that trouble to save them from the Egyptians and the Red Sea only to let them be eaten by snakes. They laughed at Dathan and Abiram, packed their belongings, and followed Moses.

But, when they reached the desert of Shur, they were horrified! Dathan and Abiram were right! For miles and miles, as far as the eye could see, there were only snakes and lizards and scorpions. Such terror! Now certainly all the people would perish!

One or two gathered courage to approach Moses with the suggestion that they turn back. But he told them not to be afraid of the snakes, just to follow him and they would be all right.

"I promise you," Moses said to all the people, "that not one of you will be harmed by the snakes."

"Then lead on, Moses," the people cried. "We will follow you!"

So Moses marched on ahead into the wilderness, with the people right behind him. As they began to approach the snakes, a marvelous thing happened! As soon as the snakes saw Moses and the Israelites, they moved to the left and moved to the right and coiled up meekly on the sand, forming a path, letting the Israelites march through without so much as stinging one person!

The people were overjoyed. But Dathan and Abiram muttered in disappointment. They were cruel enough to wish that a few people had really been harmed, just to prove themselves right. But everyone marched through untouched.

Two or three people mocked Dathan and Abiram. But they only grumbled and said, "Wait, there is worse to come. Wait till you reach Moro."

The people, with Moses at their head, marched on through the desert. At the end of three days, just when they reached Moro, their water supply ran low. Now they faced one of the worst fears of the desert, the fear of thirst.

"You see," Dathan crowed. "I told you worse things would happen. Now what can Moses do for you?"

"The water supply is almost gone," Abiram sneered. "I wonder what Moses will do to get water for you?"

Someone answered them. "Do you think Moses would have rescued us from the Egyptians, saved us from the Red Sea, led us safely through the wilderness of the snakes, and now will let us die of thirst?"

But only a few brave ones talked that way. The rest began to murmur angrily.

"Moses is a bad leader."

"Very bad, or he would not let this happen."

"And God?" said one very angry person. "What kind of a God lets the people die of thirst?"

"Sh!" a more timid person whispered. "Sh! God may hear you grumbling and punish you. Besides, we're not suffering from thirst yet."

"But we will, very soon," someone spoke up.

"Wait, wait," cried a gentle person. "There, look! What do I see? A mile away. Isn't that a spring?"

Everyone hurried forward. Yes, there were springs from which clear water was flowing! Dathan and Abiram ran ahead and drank first from the springs. But they spit out the water with angry exclamations.

"That water is bitter!" Dathan said. "You can't drink it. Try it. Taste it yourselves. You'll find it's very bitter."

Many people rushed forward, but each one did as Dathan and Abiram did. They spit out the water, some angry that it was so bitter, some worried, some sad.

"What will we drink?" someone asked.

"I would rather have been killed by the Egyptians," said one person, "than to die in the desert of thirst."

"You're right," said another. "Death from thirst is a slow, painful death. I would rather have died quickly, thrust through the heart with an Egyptian spear."

"I agree," said a third. "The real fear is not death itself, but the fear of dying."

The scheming of Dathan and Abiram and the mutterings of the people came to Moses' ears. He sighed deeply and wearily, wondering again why he had undertaken this very difficult, almost impossible task of leading the Israelites through the desert to the Promised Land. But he didn't sigh long. He did not have time for sighing. The people needed water to drink, and he must provide it quickly.

Moses prayed for help and received this answer: "Moses, take a branch of the laurel tree. On that branch write My great and glorious name. Then throw that laurel branch into the water."

Moses cut off a branch of the laurel, wrote on it as he had been instructed. Then he called the people around him and showed them the branch on which he had written the great and glorious name of God.

"I shall throw this laurel branch into the water," Moses said. "Watch. Let us see what happens."

"It's only a trick," Dathan muttered.

But the moment the laurel branch touched it, the water became sparklingly clear, and, when they tasted it, they found it sweet and wonderful to drink. And once more they were happy and satisfied to follow Moses wherever he would lead them.

"Just wait," Dathan warned them. "You haven't had any real trouble yet. Just wait. Something else is going to happen, and this time Moses won't be able to help you."

But the people were sorry they had listened to Dathan at all because, everytime serious trouble threatened, Moses found a way out.

So, cheerful once more, they marched on after Moses, singing, telling jokes, happy the whole day long. They marched on and on until one day they reached Elim.

By this time they had been out of Egypt for thirty-one days. They thought they had carried with them enough bread to eat. But, at the end of thirty-one days, their food supply was all gone.

"Now what do you think of your leader, the great Moses?" Dathan said sarcastically. "Look how poorly he planned. Here you are, only thirty-one days away from Egypt, and you have no food left."

"Yes," piped up Abiram. "Now you'll starve to death."

"Be quiet!" said one person who had defended Moses twice before. "Do you think Moses rescued us from the Egyptians, saved us from drowning in the Red Sea, led us safely through the snakes of Shur, sweetened the water at Moro, only to let us starve to death at Elim?"

But this time no one listened to him.

One group began to weep, crying, "We left Egypt, expecting freedom, and now we can't even live as slaves much less as a free people."

"At least," cried another group, "our Egyptian masters gave us food. It was only bread and water, but it kept us alive. Oh, now we shall starve!"

Another group began to shiver, whimpering, "Moses said we would be happy, but we are most unfortunate. It would have been better to have died in Egypt."

Moses heard all these complaints and now, for the first time, he grew angry. He said to Aaron, "These ungrateful people. Think of all the miracles God has already done for them. Now listen to them whine."

"But Moses, my brother," Aaron said quietly, "they are frightened. They think they are going to starve."

"Yes, yes, I know," Moses agreed. "When people are afraid, they think only of the trouble they have at this moment and forget the many times they were saved. Well, of course, I am really not too angry. I will pray again for them."

While he was praying, Dathan and Abiram went to each person, spreading the lie that Moses was helpless to find food. They wanted to start a riot. They tried to get the people to promise that, if Moses had not supplied food for them by tomorrow morning, they would desert Moses and appoint Dathan as their leader.

Some agreed. But many were unwilling to make such a decision against Moses.

"Let us wait until morning," someone said, "then we will make plans."

Dathan and Abiram were satisfied with that answer because they were certain that by morning the people would be so hungry they would agree to any wicked plan.

Everybody went to sleep.

Moses did not sleep. He spent the night praying for food.

Up in heaven there was a great hurrying and a stirring with angels flying at full speed to do God's bidding. A message was sent to the angels in the third heaven to start the manna mills working. They rushed to their work, knowing it would take all night to grind enough manna for all the Israelites. Manna was a miracle food, prepared by the angels.

All night long the angels worked hard and fast. As soon as the first batch was ready, the angels in charge of distribution went to work.

First they called to the wind to do its job. It came whistling sharply, so fast did it come. It set to work, sweeping the floor of the desert until it was clean of all surface dirt. It puffed and blew with all its might, sweeping the floor with great strong gusts.

When it finished, it billowed away.

Then came the rain to wash the floor clean so that not one speck of dirt remained. The rain started out with tiny drops, little by little bringing out bigger and bigger drops, until a solid sheet of water dashed against the floor. Every drop of dirt was washed away.

Then the rain flowed off to the sea.

Then it was time for the dew. It came down gently, in tiny specks to settle over the floor of the desert like a table. As the dew fell so gently, the wind came back and blew hard on it to freeze it. When the wind finished, the intermingled sand and dew sparkled like gold.

And onto the windswept, rain-washed, dew-sweetened sands of the desert were wafted thousands and thousands of measures of manna.

The people slept soundly all through the night, not hearing

the whistling of the wind, nor the spattering of the rain, nor the soft spreading of the dew.

But, when they woke in the morning and went outside their tents and saw the wonderful food on the glistening dew, they were speechless. They tasted it and broke into cheers and songs and prayers of thanksgiving. Never before had they tasted anything like this manna!

It didn't taste exactly like bread, nor like cake, nor like any one thing. But it tasted exactly like what the person eating it wanted to taste. It could be as tender as roast chicken or as flaky as fried fish or as sweet as the purest milk.

Now there was no more talk of rebellion. Even Dathan and Abiram forgot their conspiracy because they too had been very hungry. But, when they began to eat their manna, their portions turned into thousands of worms. They were white worms and brown worms, black and green, crawling, slimy, and sickening.

They began to weep, fearful that they would starve because they could not eat their worm-ridden manna. They wept, loudly and bitterly.

Moses watched them weep. Let them worry, he thought, then perhaps they will have less time for mischief. But finally he took pity on the two. He gave them some of his own manna which they could eat because his food remained fresh and did not become wormy.

Once more God had saved the people. They ate the manna, the bread of the angels, and sang their thanks to God.

Commentary

The house of Israel named it manna; it was like coriander seed, white, and it tasted like wafers in honey.　　　Exodus 16:31

* * *

After the parting of the Red Sea, the most memorable miracle recounted in the Exodus narrative is that of the manna, the heavenly food that appeared miraculously overnight and sustained the Israelites during their forty years of wandering in the wilderness. Not surprisingly, the manna, by its origin and nature, was a natural subject for embellishment in the Midrash. The rabbinic legends tell how the manna variously tasted like whatever one had a craving for: "Just as the infant finds many flavors in its mother's milk, so did Israel find many a taste in the manna as long as they were eating it." (*Yoma* 75a) Furthermore, the manna spoiled overnight, so it had to be eaten the day it fell. What does the falling of manna reveal? Above all, God's concern for the children of Israel, for their well-being and happiness. And what does its spoiling demonstrate? That we must appreciate and make use of the blessings that come to us now and not postpone our good intentions.

* * *

With a daily miraculous demonstration of God's concern and affection for Israel, such as with manna, it is difficult to understand what induced the people to lose faith so often in both God and Moses. Yet they did, repeatedly, especially when overcome by heat or thirst. In fact, at one point we are told that the people even sickened of the manna and complained to Moses! (Num. 21:5) This continuous restlessness and inability to accept their lot resulted, at least in part, from their having been slaves in Egypt. In servitude they were not permitted to make their own decisions; consequently, they did not have to take responsibility for themselves. Now, in the wilderness, the former slaves had to learn how to be their own masters. That is why, it is said, God decided to force them to wander for forty years. Only a new generation that did not think like slaves was worthy of entering the Promised Land.

* * *

The most serious revolt against Moses, other than that involving the incident of the Golden Calf, was the uprising led by

Korah and his followers, Dathan and Abiram. Their intention, contrary to God's divine plan, was to challenge the leadership of Moses and overthrow him. Having provoked the wrath of Moses, they were swallowed up by the earth together with their two hundred and fifty confederates in a vivid demonstration affirming God's choice of Moses as leader. (Num. 16:32–35) This point is made even more clearly in a fascinating talmudic legend about the followers of Korah. Here the talmudic sage and wanderer Rabbah bar bar Hannah, while on a caravan, is led into the desert by a mysterious Arab, who is later revealed to be Elijah. They reach a place dominated by a large crack in the earth. While Rabbah watches, the Arab takes a ball of wool, dips it in water, and puts it on his lance. Then he lowers it into the abyss for a moment. When he retrieves it, the ball is singed. Just then, Rabbah hears distant voices, repeating, "Moses is true and his Torah is true, and we are liars!" He wonders about this, and the Arab tells him it is the followers of Korah, still being punished in *Gehenna* (the Jewish equivalent of Hell). The wheel of *Gehenna* returns to that place every thirty days, and that is why they could be heard. (*Baba Batra* 74a)

Write Your Own Midrash

From where did the manna come? Was it baked in heaven by the angels? Did it come from a manna tree? Invent the source of the manna, explain how it reached the people, and also describe how it tasted to different Israelites. What happened to the manna after the Israelites entered the Promised Land? What if someone were to find the source of manna today? Would it solve all the problems of hunger and starvation in the world? Would it be shared equally by all, or would a few people try to corner the manna market? Would they succeed in doing so? If yes, would it be their right? If not, why not?

⤲6⤲

The Mountain's Reward

In the traditional Jewish view, there are no accidents in God's plan for the Israelites. They were destined to be freed from slavery by Moses, to receive the Torah, and to return to the land of Israel. From this perspective, every detail takes on great importance as a vital element in God's plan. Thus the Torah could not have been given from any mountain but Mount Sinai. Since Mount Sinai was not particularly towering or majestic, the rabbis wondered why God had selected it. This midrash answers this question.

At the foothills of Mount Tabor one day, a great Eagle and a giant Hornet settled their wings to rest. With them was the East Wind.

"Welcome, friends," the Foothills said. "You are all panting for breath. You seem quite excited. Has anything happened?"

"Oh, yes, indeed," whistled the East Wind. "Today one of the mountains in the world is going to be given a great and a wonderful reward. But let's wait until my friends, the North, South, and West Winds come, and we'll tell you the whole story."

The great Eagle spread his huge wings, almost knocking over the Hornet, and said, "You know, Friend Foothills, that I have

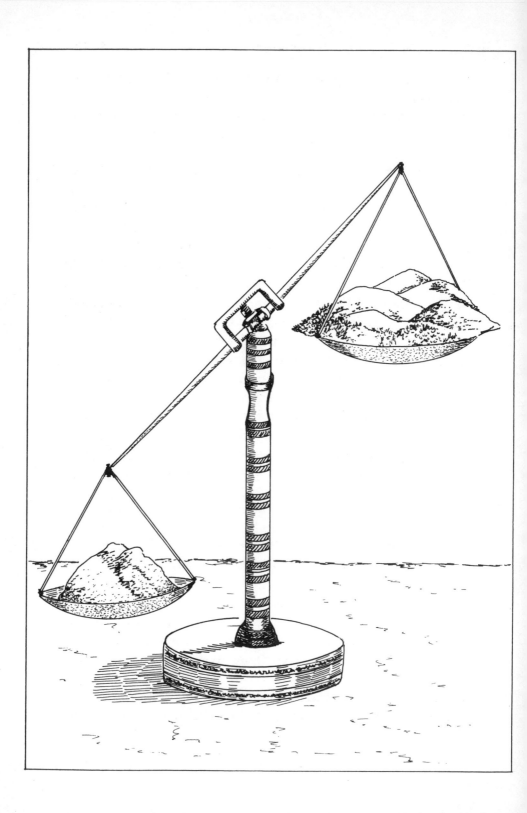

my big nest on the top of Mount Hermon. Today, while I was watching my wife teach our new little eaglet to fly, friend South Wind came whispering to me and suggested that I come and hear all about the wonderful event that is soon going to occur."

"You're exciting my curiosity," said the Foothills of Mount Tabor.

"I'm buzzing so hard," said the Hornet, "I can hardly stand still. You know, Friend Foothills, that my giant hive is at the top of Mount Carmel. Today as I was watching my baby hornets buzzing, along came the North Wind and told me what friend Eagle was told, to come here to await the news."

"Just a moment," said the Foothills. "Do I understand that Mr. Eagle is here representing Mount Hermon and that you, Mr. Hornet, are here representing Mount Carmel?"

The Eagle and the Hornet nodded.

"Well, then," said the Foothills, "I'd better call out Mrs. Ant to represent my mountain."

"But you are here to speak for Mount Tabor," the East Wind said.

"Still," the Foothills insisted, "if, as I suspect, action will have to be taken, I had better have some help. I can't move away from here, you know. Mrs. Ant will be my substitute." He raised his voice and called, "Mrs. Ant! Mrs. Ant!"

"Coming! Coming!" came back a squeaky voice, and everyone turned to watch the giant Ant come crawling through the rocks, down a tiny trail, right to the fingertips of the East Wind.

"Sh!" warned the East Wind, "I think I hear my brothers coming."

They all listened and then they all nodded as they heard a powerful rush of air from the north, from the south, and from the west. The Ant hurried to crawl under the right wing of the giant Eagle so she would not blow away, while the Hornet buzzed into safe shelter under the Eagle's left wing. The Eagle meanwhile clutched the strong arm of a well-rooted shrub with its claws, while the Winds blew into the meeting place. As soon as they settled down to a gentle sighing, the Hornet and the Ant felt it was safe to come out, and the Eagle stopped clutching the shrub.

"My, I'm out of breath," wheezed the North Wind. "Hello, everybody."

Everyone answered him and said hello to everyone else, all except the South Wind. He was looking around as if he were calling the roll.

"Everyone here?" he asked.

"No," the West Wind answered. "The big Falcon that lives on Mount Sinai isn't here. I gave him the message, but Mount Sinai said he needn't come."

"You're wrong," cried the Foothills. "Here he comes."

The Falcon came sweeping along, gasping for breath. "Am I too late?"

"Just in time!" said the East Wind.

"Attention, everyone," the North Wind commanded. "We haven't much time. Now listen. Today, on the sixth day of the third month, God is going to give to the world a wonderful gift, a very marvelous gift."

The South Wind spoke in a hushed voice. "It's the second most wonderful gift God will have given to humanity."

"What was the first?" the Ant asked timidly.

"Why, the gift of creation, the gift of life, of course!" the Falcon said sternly.

"Of course," the Eagle agreed. "Life is the most precious gift in the world."

"Well, quickly," said the Hornet, "quickly, tell us! What is this second gift?"

The Winds rustled their wings softly for a moment. Then the West Wind said, "Today God is going to give to the world . . . ," he paused for them all to get the full significance of what he was about to reveal. Then he said, "The Torah!"

"The Torah!" exclaimed the Foothills. "The book of God's Law! How marvelous a gift!"

They all began to speak at once, the Eagle and the Hornet, and the Ant and the Falcon.

"God's Torah!"

"The Law!"

"The Light of Life!"

But the North Wind silenced them quickly. "Don't take up precious time, please. I know you're all excited, but we have work to do."

But the others were too excited to be still. The Eagle asked, "To whom is it to be given?"

"We think," said the South Wind, "that it is to be given to the people of Israel."

The North Wind held up his hand. "There is no more guess-work about it, Friend South Wind. While you were busy spreading the word to the mountains in the south, God made a definite decision."

"Oh, really?" said the South Wind. "Then my news is out of date."

The North Wind nodded. He turned to the Eagle and the Hornet and the others. "All along God had wanted to give the Torah to the people of Israel."

"Then why didn't God just go ahead and do so?" the great Eagle rumbled. "Our great God doesn't have to hesitate when there is something to be done."

"True, true," said the North Wind, "but God wanted to be sure that in the future no people on earth will have cause for complaint. Suppose, without hesitation, God would give the Torah to Israel? Why, a hundred years from now, a thousand years from now, five thousand years from now, some other nation might get angry and say, 'Why was God so good to the children of Israel? If the Law had been offered to us, we would have gladly accepted it!'"

"Quite right." The East Wind fanned herself with a tiny breeze. "Everybody is so jealous of other people's good fortune, they always want all the good things for themselves. So if God would give the Torah to Israel, then later on some of the other people would be jealous and envious and hate the people of Israel. Quite right. I see your point, North Wind. Go on with your story."

"That is precisely why God wanted to give every nation on earth the chance to accept the great and wonderful Torah. So first God went to the children of Esau and said to them, 'Will you accept the Torah if I offer it to you?' And the children of Esau asked what good was the Torah. God told them, pointing out the Torah commandment 'You shall not kill.' The children of Esau just laughed at that and said, 'Oh, no, we can't be tricked out of our blessing like that!' "

"What blessing?" asked the Falcon.

"Their father Esau once received a blessing that said, 'By your sword shall you live,' which means that the tribe of Esau are hunters and raiders. Since the Torah commands them not to kill, they don't want it. So they said to God, 'No, we don't want Your Torah. You can keep it.' "

"Oh, what a dreadful thing to say to God!" The Ant shook her head in wonder. "To think they would have the nerve to say such a thing!"

The West Wind agreed. "But they weren't the only ungrateful ones. God then went to the children of Ishmael and said, 'Will you accept the Torah if I offer it to you?' "

"What did they say?" asked the Foothills.

"They wanted to know what was written in the Torah," the West Wind answered. "And when God told them that in the Torah there was a commandment 'You shall not steal,' they refused to accept it because they live by raiding other people's flocks."

"Well, I must say," said the Hornet, "that the children of Esau and Ishmael were ungrateful and stupid, to say the least."

"Oh," said the North Wind, "they weren't the only ones. God went to every people in the world and each one found some reason to refuse. But then . . . listen. . . ." There was silence for a moment. "But then God went to the people of Israel and offered the Torah to them."

"The people of Israel," said the East Wind, "asked God what was written in the Torah. When God said, 'Six hundred and thirteen commandments which you must obey,' they said, 'Very well, we will accept the Torah.'"

"But, if they didn't know what those commandments were," asked the Falcon, "why would they accept so quickly?"

"Well, the surprising thing is," said the South Wind, "that the people of Israel had been obeying many of the commandments of the Torah long before they knew they were commandments."

"Certainly," said the East Wind. "Jacob obeyed the commandments, 'I am your God'; 'you shall have no other gods before Me,' by telling his sons not to worship idols."

"Even his grandfather, Abraham," said the West Wind, "obeyed the commandment 'You shall not bear false witness,' for he was a true witness when he taught that God is the Creator of the whole world."

"And Isaac," said the South Wind, "when he was just a boy, followed the commandment to 'honor your father and your mother.' When his father wanted to bind him on the altar and give him as a sacrifice, Isaac did not refuse because he honored his father and, whatever his father ordered him to do, he would do."

"Don't forget," the East Wind spoke up quickly, "that one of Jacob's sons obeyed the commandment 'You shall not kill.' At first, when Judah and his brothers wanted to get rid of Joseph, they were going to kill him; then Judah persuaded his brothers not to kill Joseph but to sell him to the Midianites."

"And Joseph himself," and the North Wind, "obeyed the commandment to remember the Sabbath day and keep it holy even when he was a slave in Egypt. He avoided working on the Sabbath day."

"Many of the commandments were already obeyed by the people of Israel," said the West Wind. "So, when God asked them to accept the whole Torah, they were willing and glad."

"Very fine, very fine," said the Eagle. "They proved that they deserved to be given the Law. But where is it to be given?"

"Ah!" The North Wind smiled. "That's why we're here. God will give the Torah to the people of Israel," he spoke slowly for emphasis, "on the top of one of the mountains."

The Eagle and the Hornet, the Foothills and the Ant all began to shout at one time.

"Mount Hermon," shouted the Eagle.

"Mount Carmel," yelled the Hornet.

"Mount Tabor," rumbled the Foothills.

Each one wanted its mountain to be the honored one. Only the Falcon was silent. Only the Falcon did not shout for its mountain.

"Quiet! Quiet!" whistled the West Wind. One by one they fell silent. "Don't do your pleading with us. We have no power to decide. That is why we called you all together, to tell you, so you could go and ask God to let your mountain be the chosen one. Every mountain in the world is sending its representative to heaven. Now come, there's no time to lose. My brothers and I will transport all of you. Eagle, you go with North Wind. Hornet, you go with South Wind. Ant, you go with East Wind. And the Falcon will go with me."

The Falcon smiled and hung back. "Oh, I don't think there's any need for me to go. There are so many great and huge mountains in the world. Surely God will choose one of them. Mount Sinai is so small. My mountain would never be chosen."

"Don't stay here arguing," urged the West Wind. "There's no time to lose. And there's no harm in going, is there? Come, Falcon, sit in the palm of my right hand, and I'll whisk you up to heaven."

"Hurry back," shouted the Foothills, "and tell me what happens!"

"We will," the four Winds all whistled together.

And away they went in a great rush of air, right through all the heavens until they reached the Throne of Glory.

A great crowd of animals and birds was already there, each representing one of the world's mountains. The Owl was there, and the Snail, the Chipmunk, the Bird of Paradise, and many, many others.

When the four winds set down their friends, the Eagle and the Hornet and the Ant, afraid that some mountain would be chosen before they had a chance to plead for their own, pushed and shoved and crowded till they got right up to the front row. But the Falcon stayed behind, perching himself in the last row.

All was quiet. The birds and the animals, in God's presence, were humble and full of awe. There was only a gentle whispering, more the fluttering of angels' wings than anything else. Then, in a moment, even that gentle sound faded away, and, in the sudden and absolute quiet, God spoke.

"Today, I your God shall give to the children of Israel the gift of My great and holy Torah. It shall be presented to them upon the height of one of the mountains of the earth."

All the animals and birds and beasts pushed forward a little. When the great Eagle, in the first row, raised his head, all the others fell back.

"O God," solemnly said the Eagle, "I speak for Mount Hermon. Upon the height of this great mountain should You bestow the Torah to Israel. I have heard it told by my grandfather, the old Eagle, that, when Israel wished to pass through the Red Sea, it was Mount Hermon who settled down between the two shores of the sea and the people moved from one side to the other."

Almost before he was through speaking, the Ant piped up in her squeaky voice. "Please, please, God. You should choose the great Mount Tabor because long ago, in the days of Noah, when the Flood came over the earth, all the mountains in the world were covered with water except Mount Tabor. Oh, no, Mount Tabor towered high above the waters!"

Now the Hornet spoke up with a rush. "But it is Mount Carmel whom You should choose, O God. Mount Carmel rests on the mainland and on the sea. It covers land and water. It is the one worthy of Your choice."

Before anyone else could speak, God silenced them all, saying, "Did My Mount Sinai send no representation?"

"Yes, yes, indeed," said the Eagle and the Hornet and the Ant, and someone in the rear pushed the Falcon forward.

The Falcon said, "I, O God, am the representative of Mount Sinai."

"Why did you not come forward?" God asked gently. "Why do you not speak up for your mountain?"

"O high and mighty God," the Falcon answered, "Your Mount Sinai did not even wish to be represented here today. It said to me, 'Do not go, my Falcon, for I am only a small and humble little mountain, and unworthy. God would never choose me.' Therefore, O God, I was shy about coming forward when I heard of the great and wonderful deeds which these other mountains have performed. I knew my mountain would never be chosen."

"Mount Sinai is modest and humble," God answered. "I wish the people of Israel to learn this great lesson of modesty and humility. Sinai is a clean mountain. Never has anyone raised hands in worship to false gods on its heights. Nor has anyone bowed low to idols in its valleys. Sinai remains clean and pure. Thus, I choose Mount Sinai!"

The Falcon bowed low. "Oh, I thank You, God. I thank You for this gracious blessing."

All the birds and beasts and animals, helped by the North, the South, the East, and the West Winds, returned to earth to their mountains to tell them that Sinai had been chosen. Of them all, only the Falcon was happy, winging its way through the clear sunlight, singing a joyous song, to tell Mount Sinai that on its heights was the Torah to be given to Israel.

As the Falcon flew earthward, the multitudes of Israelites marched slowly to the foot of the mountain to receive the Law of God at Sinai. And God's words echoed in the stillness: "I, your God, choose Sinai because this mountain is humble and pure."

Commentary

The Lord came from Sinai.   Deuteronomy 33:2

* * *

According to the rabbis, the giving of the Torah at Mount Sinai was the turning point in world history. Not only did the Jews benefit from this great gift from God, but all nations shared in its blessings. In "The Mountain's Reward," a midrashic fable, the mountains compete for the honor of being the site upon which the Torah is given to Moses. The case for each mountain is represented by an animal. Ultimately, Mount Sinai is selected because of its modesty, reinforcing the rabbinic ethic that modesty is one of the highest virtues, thus providing an answer to the question of why an unimposing mountain was chosen by God to host so crucial an event.

* * *

In the original midrash, found in *Midrash Tehillim* (Midrash on Psalms 68:9), the vying mountains presented their own cases, emphasizing height. Mount Tabor, for example, insists that "not even the waters of the deluge overwhelmed me." Mount Carmel claims that it put itself in the middle of the Red Sea (Reed Sea) to help the Israelites cross over and escape from the Egyptians. As this is a false claim, God quickly eliminates this mountain. Finally God, quoting a passage from Isaiah 57:15, justifies the choice of Mount Sinai: *I dwell on high, in holiness; yet with the contrite and the lowly in spirit.*

*   *   *

The format of this allegorical tale is typical of rabbinic texts. A famous example, found in *Zohar* 1:2b–3b, the central text of Jewish mysticism, is the midrash in which each letter of the Hebrew alphabet appears before God arguing that it should have the honor of being the first. Each supports its argument by naming a positive word that begins with it. God turns down each letter in turn by naming a negative word that starts with the same letter. Finally the letter *alef* is selected because of its modesty.

Write Your Own Midrash

Try writing a dialogue between inanimate objects you like (e.g., animals, cars, trees, nations, etc.). Let each argue on its own behalf. Then select a winner, basing your decision on criteria other than size and strength. Choose such virtues that the rabbis endorsed as modesty and compassion.

✴ 7 ✴

Above the Mountain Top

Moses climbed Mount Sinai to receive the Torah and remained there for forty days and nights, a very long time both for Moses and for the people below who were anxiously awaiting his return. As the rabbis wondered how Moses sustained himself during that long ascent, many legends developed to describe the time Moses spent on Mount Sinai, where, according to the Torah, he was closer to God than anyone has been before or since. One of these legends, found in the Talmud, explains that Moses did not remain on the top of the mountain but ascended into Paradise and there received the Torah. This may explain his lack of need for sustenance during that long period, but it raises new questions concerning what happened to him in the heavens: How was he, a mortal, treated by the angels? How did they feel about the giving of the Torah? All of these questions are answered in this story, which is based on the talmudic text.

The place and the people were now selected. From Mount Sinai, Israel was to receive the Law, and Moses, their leader, prepared to climb the mountain slopes. Joshua was to go part way up the mountain with him.

When they reached the first plateau, Moses turned to Joshua and said, "You will wait here for me. I shall climb up into the clouds at the top of the mountain."

"O dear Master," Joshua begged, "let me go with you."

"No, no. Here is where you remain."

Joshua obediently stayed behind on the plateau and watched Moses climb up and up until he disappeared into the clouds.

In the loneliness of the mountain top, for seven days, Moses stayed by himself, calming his mind, preparing his heart, trying to be as perfect as a human being could be that he might be worthy to receive the Law.

At twilight on the seventh day, he said to himself, "I am very tired. Perhaps I shall sleep for a few moments."

It was quiet on the mountain. Moses looked at the white clouds floating above him, seeming so close that he wanted to reach out and touch one. He sighed, closed his eyes, and fell fast asleep. While he slept, he dreamed.

A large, gray cloud had settled on the mountain top. And out of the cloud came a whisper, "Wake up, Moses. Wake up. I've come to take you through fire."

"Who spoke to me?" Moses cried out.

"I did," said the cloud. "Come here to me. Before you receive the Torah, you must challenge the fires of heaven."

"What talk is this!" Moses exclaimed. "I go through the fires in heaven? How could I get to heaven? God sent no chariot for me."

"I am the chariot," the cloud said. "Come, do not waste anymore time. You mortals spend so much time talking that it's a wonder you ever get anything done in the world."

"Don't be so stormy," Moses said. "You must realize it upsets a mortal to have a cloud suddenly talk with human words." Then, quickly, when he saw the cloud drift impatiently, he said, "I'm ready to come with you, but I don't know what to do. Shall I ride on top of you, or shall I just hold onto one of your edges?"

"Come, come," said the cloud impatiently. "My mouth is open. Just walk in and make yourself at home."

Moses walked right into the mouth of the cloud and found that the gray and fleecy material was soft and pleasant to stand on. But, as the cloud began to lift away from the mountain up into the air, Moses rocked back and forth. Because he was getting dizzy, he sat down. His dizziness passed, and then he rode more comfortably.

Just when it seemed as though they must have reached the very highest heaven and would go right on through the ceiling, the cloud stopped. Moses heard a loud voice, "Hold on! Who goes there?"

He poked his head out of the cloud's mouth and saw an angel. "Who are you?" he asked.

"I am Kemuel, the porter-angel."

"He's the angel in charge of the twelve thousand Angels of Destruction," the cloud whispered to Moses.

But, before Moses could even open his mouth in surprise, Kemuel said, "What are you doing here in this spot? This place belongs to the Angels of Fire."

"God sent this cloud to bring me," said Moses. "I am here to receive the Torah for the people of Israel."

"Oh!" Kemuel shouted. "You'll take our Torah away from us, will you? Oh, no! You shall not pass!"

Suddenly Moses found himself in a fight and, to his surprise, succeeded to push the angel aside. Moses hurried back into the mouth of the cloud, urging the cloud to speed on.

On they went until they were stopped by the angel Hadarniel. Kemuel had not frightened Moses, but Hadarniel did. He was so big, so huge. Moses had never seen anything that big, not even a mountain, and, from his mouth as he talked, thousands of burning lightning flashes poured out.

Hadarniel roared, the lightning flashes reaching out to burn Moses.

"Who are you? And what are you doing in this high and holy place?"

Now Moses was too frightened to answer him. Any moment he expected the fire to lick out and burn him. He just stood and trembled. Then God called down, "Cease, Hadarniel, cease. This is My servant Moses. I have called him here to receive the Torah. Why do you frighten him?"

Now it was Hadarniel's turn to tremble. And he cried out quickly, "O Most High, I did not know that he was here at Your bidding. I am glad to welcome him; in fact, I will be his guide."

Moses went back inside the cloud, and, with Hadarniel to lead them, they went on until they reached the fire of Sandalfon. Hadarniel said to Moses, "Here I must leave you. If I try to go forward, the fires of Sandalfon will scorch me."

With a twist of his wings, spurting flame from his mouth, he turned and was soon gone from sight, leaving Moses more terrified than ever because Sandalfon was now the hugest thing he had ever seen! Sandalfon was so tall that, if someone could walk up his height, it would take five hundred years to get from his feet to his head. Moses was so frightened he almost fell out of the cloud.

"Careful, Moses, hang on," the cloud muttered, not too happy himself to be so near the fire.

"What shall I do now?" cried Moses. "Oh, I shall surely be consumed by the fire."

"Do not fear, Moses," God called down. "Continue on. You shall be safe."

So Moses went past Sandalfon, then past the Rigyon, which is a river of fire, until he came almost to the Throne of Glory. There he met the Angels of Terror. The strongest and the mightiest of all, they surrounded the Throne of Glory.

They reached out to scorch Moses with their breaths of fire, but God said to Moses, "Hold on tightly to the Throne of My Glory, and they will not harm you."

The chief Angels of Heaven, the seraphim and cherubim, hovered near Moses, who trembled in terror. But they did not try to harm him as long as he held onto the Throne of Glory. However, they were annoyed and perplexed.

One of them said to God, "What is this earthly creature doing here?"

"He has come to receive My Torah."

Another angel stepped forward and said, "O God, what do You need with this mortal made of dust? Are You not satisfied with us, Your celestial creatures?"

"Oh, yes, God," cried out another angel. "Why don't You leave the Torah with us?"

God nodded to Moses, thus giving him permission to answer the angels if he wished.

Moses turned nervously to them, not knowing if he could possibly convince them by human words. But, since God was remaining silent, Moses understood that it was his duty to try. His mind cast about for the right words, but the angels standing around him were so fearful looking that he stood speechless.

Then he remembered the people of Israel and how they were waiting for him to bring God's gift to them. His mind cleared suddenly. He knew what to say.

"If You, O God, will permit me to speak . . ."

Moses turned to the Angels of Terror. "In the Torah it is written, 'You shall have no other gods but Me.' Is it possible that, among you angels, there could be even one idol worshiper?"

"Of course not!" one of the angels answered indignantly.

"Then you do not need that law against idol worship." Moses continued. "In the Torah it is written, 'Honor your father and your mother.' Do you, perhaps, have parents?"

The angels looked at each other and did not answer.

"Then what use is this law to you?" Moses asked. "In the Torah it is written, 'You shall not kill.' Is there any chance that among you there may be a murderer?"

"Of course not!" chorused the angels.

"Then this law is useless to you." Now Moses grew bolder. He said, "Surely you have no thieves among the angels. 'You shall not steal' is written in the Torah. You have no money in heaven, so what could you steal from one another?"

Moses went on, presenting one argument after another, giving an example with each commandment to prove why the angels had no need for the Torah. Then, like a good advocate, he summed up his case with a winning argument.

He said, "You angels are pure. There is no sin among you. God's Law is not for angels. But we creatures who live on earth, we steal, lie, cheat, and murder. These poor, weak mortals, these sinful people, *they* need the Torah."

The leader of the angels stepped forward. He looked at Moses and said, "You have convinced us. The people of the earth need the Torah."

Moses bowed, modest but happy in his victory. Then he said, "Thank you. I thank you, and the children of Israel thank you."

Moses let go of the Throne of Glory, stepped into the cloud, and felt himself wafted down through the heavens.

With a soft bump of his hand on his knee, he roused himself and opened his eyes. He looked around and saw that he was still sitting on the mountain top, and the white clouds were drifting overhead. He smiled.

"What an interesting vision," he said. "It seemed that I went up into heaven and quarreled with the angels about the Torah. Very interesting. Won't Joshua be amazed when I tell him?"

Moses then spent the rest of his time on the mountain in meditation and study, writing down the thoughts that came to his heart. After a while, he said to himself, "Now I believe I have cast out of my mind every mean thought I may ever have had. I believe I have cast out of my heart every evil feeling I ever had. Now I believe I am ready to receive the Torah."

For forty days he stayed there, communing with God, learning about the Law. At the end of that time, clutching the Torah to his breast, he left the mountain top and marched down towards the camps of Israel, bringing to the people the holy Torah, the word of God.

Commentary

Moses approached the thick cloud where God was.

Exodus 20:18

*   *   *

According to the Midrash, the Torah was given to humans over the objections of the angels, who asked, *"What is man that You have been mindful of him?"* (Ps. 8:5) This tradition is the basis for the midrash in which Moses ascends into Paradise in order to receive the Torah but has to plea for God's help when the angels try to expel him. This story is intended to show the preciousness of the Torah, even to the angels. At the same time, it emphasizes that the Torah is meant for human beings. These points are proven when Moses asks the angels if any of the Ten Commandments are relevant to them, and they admit that they are not.

*   *   *

The idea of an ascent into Paradise takes many forms in ancient Jewish literature. In the Bible only Elijah, who is carried into heaven in a chariot of fire, reaches this sacred world. But in legends others make the journey as well. Enoch, for example, is transported into heaven, in a similar manner, in a mystical chariot known as the *Merkavah*. In a talmudic legend (*Hagigah* 14b), four sages journey to Paradise. Rabbi Akiba ben Joseph, Simeon ben Azzai, Simeon ben Zoma, and Elisha ben Abuyah enter *Pardes,* literally an orchard but here understood as referring to Paradise. Of the four, Ben Azzai "looked and died," Ben Zoma "looked and lost his mind," Elisha ben Abuyah "cut the shoots"—meaning that he lost his faith—and only Rabbi Akiba entered and departed in peace. In some very early Jewish writing about heavenly journeys, known as hechalot texts (*hechalot* refers to the palace of heaven), the adventures of Rabbi Ishmael and others are described in great detail. Whether those who wrote these texts believed them to be literally true or understood them as parable is not known.

* * *

In another talmudic legend (*Hagigah* 13b) the angel Sandalfon is described as weaving the prayers of Israel into garlands of prayer for God to wear while sitting on the Throne of Mercy. (Rabbinic legend holds that God has two thrones in heaven, a Throne of Justice and a Throne of Mercy.) While on the Throne of Justice, God sometimes makes decisions that are harsh, as when God destroyed the world in the time of the Flood or destroyed the cities of Sodom and Gomorrah. But, when sitting on the Throne of Mercy, God's judgments are merciful. The legend of the garland woven by Sandalfon links the prayers of Israel with the mercy of God.

Write Your Own Midrash

Write a midrash about a heavenly journey. Decide what method to reach Paradise will be used—Jacob's ladder, a magic amulet, the pronunciation of God's name, the heavenly chariot, or some other vehicle. Then describe your vision of Paradise. There are many rabbinic legends about this, such as those found in *Everyman's Talmud* by A. Cohen. Describe the angels and how they treat the visitor, who can be anyone you wish. For example, there are legends about Isaac's ascent to heaven from the altar on Mount Moriah. There are also legends about the ascent into Paradise of Enoch, Elijah, Rabbi Akiba, and Rabbi Ishmael, among others.

✥8✥

The Broken Tablets

The long absence of Moses on Mount Sinai raised grave doubts in the minds of the Israelites about his fate and about the wisdom of their seemingly endless wandering through the wilderness. As their doubts and hysteria grew, they abandoned their faith in Moses and God and created an idol out of the gold and jewels they had taken with them from Egypt. This was the Golden Calf, which the people were worshiping as Moses descended from Mount Sinai with the Tablets of the Law in his hands.

I t was the morning of the forty-first day. On the plateau Joshua faced the mountain, peering upward anxiously, waiting for Moses to appear.

The strong light of the morning stung his eyes. He protected them with his hand, trying to see against the glare. Far away in the distance he saw a moving dot. In a few minutes it grew larger, and he realized that it must be Moses. He began to run forward, up the rocky path. Now he could see Moses clearly. He was slowly descending the steep hill, carrying two stone tablets!

"Master!" Joshua called out. "O my teacher, I am glad to see you."

As he reached him, Moses stopped to rest, and Joshua said, "The tablets! You bring the Tablets of the Law!"

"Yes," Moses said quietly, smiling.

Joshua held out his arms. "They are heavy. Let me carry them."

"No, thank you, Joshua," Moses said, not loosening his hold on them. "They are heavy, but I shall continue to carry them. I am to give them to the *whole* people and not to one person alone, not even to you, my faithful pupil."

Joshua nodded. He ran the tips of his fingers over the columns of stone. He and Moses smiled at each other happily. Then he put his hand under Moses' elbow to ease the weight.

"Now that you have come with the Law of God," he said, "all is well again. But I have been anxious for your return."

"And are the people of Israel waiting so eagerly for the Law, too?" Moses asked.

"Oh, yes. Ever since dawn I have heard shouting and singing from the direction of our camp. I am sure they are waiting for you. And I have waited since before dawn. When you did not come, I began to worry that you had fallen ill and could not get word to me. I even imagined that a wild animal had attacked you!"

Moses smiled. "You young people have no patience. It takes a long time to descend from the high crest of Mount Sinai. Come, Joshua, forward. The people wait impatiently. Let us hurry."

So Moses carried the Tablets of the Law, and the two men worked their way down the mountain. Everything around them took part in this happy occasion. The air became crystal clear. Birds trilled sweet songs. Bushes parted their thick branches to let them through without a scratch. Stones rolled aside so their feet would not be bruised. All of nature joined to hasten the coming of the Law to Israel. So they walked along with light steps and happy hearts.

As they walked, they talked. The closer they came to the camp, the louder the shouting sounded.

Joshua said, "It sounds as if the people are praying."

"Oh, no," Moses answered. "That's not the way to pray. We don't have to shout. We pray quietly."

"In Egypt," Joshua said, "when I heard the heathens pray, they always shouted and yelled. Why didn't they pray quietly, as we do?"

"False idols are made of wood and stone," Moses said, "and cannot hear. People shout at them hoping somehow to make those lifeless things hear. But, when *we* pray, we may do so in low murmurs, or if we wish, silently, even without moving our lips. God knows what is in our hearts. We don't need to shout."

So they talked as they walked until they reached the lower foothills of the mountain. Then, suddenly, everything changed. The songs of the birds stopped abruptly. The clear air faded into mist. Their steps were heavy, and strangely the joy of carrying their precious burden faded and a gloom entered their hearts. In the distance they heard noises of shouting and yelling, growing stronger and louder.

"Hear that shouting," Joshua said, puzzled. "It's different from what I heard earlier. Some enemy must have invaded our camp."

"Oh, no," Moses answered sadly. "Those are not war cries. Don't you remember that noise from Egypt? It sounds like the yelling of a mob dancing in the presence of an idol."

"False idols!" Joshua exclaimed. "That can't be!"

"That's just what it sounds like," Moses said, "the noises people make when worshiping an idol. Oh, something must be very wrong. Hurry, Joshua. Let us hurry and see what has happened."

Almost running now, they hurried down to the desert, where the Israelites were encamped.

At first all they could see was a huge fire around which the people were dancing, yelling, and shouting. Moses pushed through the mob, elbowing people aside. They were so excited they did not look at him. They must have thought he was one of them, trying to get closer to the fire and the new god they had fashioned in his absence.

In time Moses worked his way through hundreds of people to the inner circle. And there, in front of him, he saw Aaron, held prisoner by Jannes and Jambres.

He lifted his eyes from the three men. There beyond them on a high pedestal with the sun gleaming on it, making it shoot off little sparkles, was a calf made of gold!

Anger so great and so terrible shook Moses that, when he spoke, his voice thundered.

"Aaron!" Moses' thunderous voice rang out over the yelling of the mob.

At that great shout every other voice fell silent. Moses turned to the people with a face so terrifying to see that those nearest him crushed back against those behind them, trying to get away from his anger.

"Aaron!" Moses thundered. "Who made this idol of gold?"

Now the silence was broken by frightened whimperings.

"It is Moses!"

"He is not dead!"

"That vision was false!"

"He carries two tablets!"

"It is Moses!"

"Quiet!" Moses thundered. "Silence! You fools, you miserable fools!"

His voice broke, and for a moment he could not go on. When he did, his voice was quieter. So silent was the mob that even a whisper would have been heard.

"Poor, wretched fools. Aaron, my brother, tell me, who made this idol?"

Aaron's voice quivered. "O Moses, we saw a vision in which you lay dead, and we feared the Law was lost to us forever. The people begged me, they wanted some god to worship."

"They wanted!" Moses said scornfully. "They wanted! Weak, foolish people! But you, my brother Aaron, were you weak, too?"

"We would have killed him," Jannes shouted, "if he had tried to stop us."

"Just as we killed Hur!" Jambres cried.

Moses raised his hand to strike the two brothers, then, controlling himself, dropped it to his side. He turned to the people.

"You stupid people! You wicked fools! Oh, I cannot begin to tell you the depths of your folly! Was it not you whom our God had chosen? Has God not given you the greatest treasure? For forty days you were to wait, that's all, just forty days. But you couldn't wait. You couldn't wait forty days. Oh, no, you wanted an idol made of gold. Very well then, if you did not want the Law, you shall not have it!" His voice rose to thunder again. "Neither the Law nor that calf!"

Before anyone could guess what he would do, Moses raised the two tablets of stone high above his head, then swung them down fast, smashing them against a rock. They broke into hundreds of little pieces.

"The Law!"

"He smashed the Holy Tablets!"

Moses did not heed these cries, but he reached down, picked up a heavy stone, and, with all his might, threw it at the Golden Calf. The idol shook on its foundation, tottered, fell to the ground with a crash, and broke into thousands of pieces.

The noise rolled like thunder over the silent multitude. Then quietly, without a word, the people moved backward, away from the broken calf, away from the broken tablets, away from the majestic rage of Moses, their leader.

Without speaking, without a glance, Moses turned his back. With bent head and bowed shoulders, he stumbled slowly to his tent.

After a few hours passed, Aaron and Joshua came to stand humbly before him. They pleaded with him. First they whispered to him, then they spoke more loudly.

"Beg God to forgive them," Aaron pleaded.

"They were foolish," Joshua begged, "but ask for forgiveness."

Moses' voice was cold and hard. "I have been praying. Yes, even though the people were wicked, I have cried aloud for pardon. But this time, I am afraid that God will not easily forgive. Leave me in peace. Let me pray again."

The long night hours dragged by. At dawn Aaron and Joshua returned, again begging Moses to plead with God for forgiveness.

"This sin is too great," he said sadly. "How can you or I or anyone expect that it will ever be pardoned? The Law has written in it, 'I am your God; you shall have no other gods besides Me.' Yet, at the very moment when I was bringing them the Law, they fashioned an idol of gold. Oh, no, no, I believe that never can they be forgiven!"

With tears in his eyes, Aaron said, "But you must try, Moses. Try! The people weep for their very lives! They know now they have sinned, and they are sorry. They repent, and they ask for pardon."

Moses shook his head but did not refuse. He sent them away and then tried again to win forgiveness for the people. For two whole hours Moses begged, but God refused. Then finally God told Moses what the people could do to be forgiven. After listening carefully, Moses sent for Aaron and Joshua, telling them to bring Bezalel and Oholiab.

To these four men Moses explained what the people of Israel must now do. Of this new task, the heavy work would fall on Bezalel, who was a builder, and his assistant, Oholiab. When these two men agreed to help, they, Moses, Aaron, and Joshua went to speak to the people.

The multitude stood with bowed heads, waiting for Moses to speak.

"For long hours," Moses said slowly and quietly, "I have been praying. For long hours has God refused to hearken to my plea. But our God is merciful and will forgive you."

The people raised their heads slowly, but they did not dare even to whisper their joy.

"But," Moses warned, "you will be forgiven only if you learn, at last, how to worship God."

"We will worship God everywhere," cried one person.

"In field and in forest," called another.

"In the valleys and on the mountains," cried a third.

"At home and on the road," shouted still another.

"Good," Moses answered slowly. "That is good. You may worship God wherever you wish because God is everywhere."

"We will!" the people called in one voice.

Moses held up his hand. "God can be worshiped in the silence of the heart as well as in the spoken word. But, in order that you do not again forget, God wishes you to build a sacred place on earth, a sanctuary."

Aaron spoke up. "But, if we worship God always and everywhere, why do we need a temple?"

"You forgot God once on the road and in your camp," Moses said. "Instead you built a golden calf to worship."

The people shuffled their feet in embarrassment.

"If you build a tabernacle for God, there you will go regularly to worship, and you will not forget God again."

"Then let us build this sanctuary quickly," Joshua said.

"One more word," Moses said. "There is one other reason why you are commanded to build this tabernacle. It will be a sign to the other people of the world that God has forgiven you."

Now the people began to hold their heads high.

"When we have the tabernacle in which to worship God," Aaron said, "we shall be happy again. But, O Moses, what of the Law? What of the tablets that you broke?"

Moses sighed deeply. "Yes, what of the Law? Ah! That I cannot say. We must pray and hope that, if we follow God's instructions in the building of the sanctuary, perhaps some day

God will forgive us completely by giving us the Law again. But that I cannot promise. I can only hope. It depends on you. Let us build this temple as God commands."

"We will, Moses," the people cried, "we will build!"

"With what will you build?" asked Moses. "You used up your treasures for the Golden Calf."

"There is more treasure in our tents," they shouted.

"There is still gold!"

"There is still silver!"

"There is fine linen."

"And precious wood."

Moses smiled and nodded. "Then bring it all to Bezalel whose skilled hands will build God's tabernacle."

The people left, but they returned quickly, bringing their remaining treasures. The work started at once.

When the sanctuary was completed, Moses disappeared for a short time. When he returned, he summoned the people and said, "This I declare to be the Day of Atonement, the day on which you repent fully and completely for your sins. The sin of worshiping a false god is the worst you can commit. Therefore, spend the day in fasting and in prayer. When the Day of Atonement comes to an end, then will God forgive you."

The hours of the morning passed quickly. The early afternoon hours wore away. But the late hours of the day lagged and went slowly. Finally the Day of Atonement came to a close.

Then Moses rose before the people and spoke.

"These words which now I speak come directly from God. Listen closely.

" 'Between Me and My children, there was anger. Between us, there was enmity. Between us there was hatred. Now there is friendship, love, and peace.' "

As Moses paused, the deep silence was broken by a sigh.

"Now," said Moses softly, "God has forgiven your sins."

But quickly, before the people would separate and scatter to their tents, Aaron spoke.

"But, O brother Moses, what of the Law?"

"Yes, yes," the people cried. "The Law!"

Then Moses pushed aside the curtain that covered the ark and brought forth two tablets of stone.

"These are the new tablets which I have brought again from Mount Sinai for you."

He held them out to the people.

"Here is God's Law. Guard it well. Study it always. Live by its commandments. And that you forget not your sin, the broken pieces of the first tablets will be kept in the ark with the new Tablets of the Law."

Commentary

As soon as Moses came near the camp and saw the calf and the dancing, he became enraged; and he hurled the tablets from his hands and shattered them at the foot of the mountain.

Exodus 32:19

* * *

The long-suffering, now liberated children of Israel were singled out by God to receive the Torah. But, at that very moment, they seem to have lost faith and constructed the Golden Calf. From a midrashic perspective, this ranks as the most serious transgression since the Fall of Adam and Eve. The rabbis, therefore, sought an explanation of the Israelites' unfaithfulness both to Moses and God. As in the tale of Eve and the serpent (Gen. 3), the blame is assigned to Satan (closely identified with the serpent), who is said in the Midrash to have shown the people a vision of Moses lying dead, which caused panic and loss of faith among them and led to the Golden Calf incident. In the Exodus story, the former slaves repeatedly lose faith in Moses. At one point the people even complain that they are tired of the manna, the miraculous food from heaven. In response, a furious God unleashes fiery serpents to punish them.

* * *

The most dangerous time in a major undertaking is the moment before its completion. That, according to the rabbis, is when the Evil Impulse, known as *Yetzer Hara,* is most powerful. The rabbis explained that every person has such an evil impulse (as well as a good impulse, known as *Yetzer Hatov*). These two forces struggle against one another: sometimes one holds sway, sometimes the other. The Evil Impulse serves evil, as represented by Satan. In one midrash Satan appears in disguise to stop Abraham from sacrificing Isaac, fearing that Abraham's act of faith would bring the Messiah, thus defeating all of Satan's efforts to delay the Messianic Age. (Genesis Rabbah 56:4)

* * *

The rabbis speculated for generations as to the contents of the first set of tablets that were given to Moses, assuming that the second tablets differed in some elementary way from the first. Some say that the content of the first tablets was composed entirely of positive commandments while the second emphasized the negative. Other legends, especially those found in the *Zohar,* the key text of medieval Jewish mysticism, suggest that the letters were not carved on the first tablets but fluttered on them like black fire on white fire. And, when Moses cast the tablets down, the letters flew back to heaven and away from the human realm. This image of the flying letters reappears in Jewish lore in the Yiddish tale of a town of sinners who discovered one day that their scroll of the Torah had become blank. A scribe in a nearby town woke the same morning to discover that the blank Torah scroll he was about to write was suddenly complete, from the first letter to the last.

Write Your Own Midrash

Write a midrash about the first tablets, which Moses broke. What were the Ten Commandments like? How do they differ from those of the second tablets? What did the first tablets look like? In the *Zohar* they were described as black fire on white fire, flying to heaven when the tablets were broken. How do you imagine them? Did the first tablets contain great secrets that were lost? What kinds of secrets? Were the first tablets really broken or did something else happen to them (e.g., a hand came down from heaven to take them back)?

♦ 9 ♦

The Rod of Almonds

When the time came to select the tribe of the High Priest of Israel, every tribe desired this great honor. Moses knew that the High Priest would be Aaron, whose role in liberating the Jews from Egyptian bondage had been second only to Moses himself. But it was clear that the people would accept this decision only if it came from God and not from Moses. Therefore Moses had each tribe bring a rod to the Tent of the Pact and leave it there overnight. The next day, when they looked inside, they discovered that a miracle had taken place—one of the rods had sprouted blossoms. This was God's way of indicating from which tribe the High Priest should come.

Four sentries stood guard at the Treasure Tent. Two marched back and forth in front of the entrance, two guarded it from the rear. In the still night only the sound of their voices and their footsteps disturbed the quiet.

Dathan and Abiram were hidden in the shadows, and to them the alertness of the sentries was a danger. The two men stared unwinkingly into the gloom, watching the soldiers, waiting for them to relax their guard. Dathan and Abiram were here to sneak into the Treasure Tent to steal the precious jewels which had been brought there that noon for safekeeping.

Dathan moved impatiently, to make a daring rush, but Abiram held him back. One hour passed and the guards walked their post. Then, as the second hour dragged along, Dathan decided on a bold dash. At that moment, the two rear-guard sentries, disobeying orders, strolled over to speak to the soldiers in the front.

Quickly Abiram and Dathan sprang from the shadows, darted to the tent, and noiselessly and swiftly worked their way under the canvas, without the soldiers being the wiser. At first, the tent appeared to be dark inside. Then, as their eyes became accustomed to the light, they were able to see a few objects in the tent. Through an occasional pinhole in the canvas, the moon shone onto the jewels sparkling on their velvet cushions, bringing a faint glow of light.

The two thieves, afraid to talk except in whispers, and only when necessary, crept from cushion to cushion examining the precious stones lying there.

That morning Moses had ordered the leaders of each of the twelve tribes to bring the jewel of the tribe to the Treasure Tent. These gems were to be placed in the breastplate of the High Priest. On the next day when Moses would appoint Aaron as High Priest of Israel, this brilliant breastplate was to hang over his priestly robes.

Now as Dathan and Abiram tiptoed through the Treasure Tent looking at the precious gems, they muttered under their breath.

"Here is the ruby from Reuben's tribe," Dathan whispered. "And the smaragd from Simeon's."

"Look at the beautiful emerald from the tribe of Judah," Abiram said, "and the carbuncle of Levi's tribe."

"Ah," breathed Dathan, "see, the blue sapphire from Issachar and the white pearl of Zebulun."

"Look how the moonlight brings out the delicate lights of the topaz of Dan and the turquoise of Naphtali," Abiram whispered, smoothing the velvet on which the stones lay. "And the crystal of Gad's tribe and from Asher's the chrysolite."

"See this onyx of Joseph's tribe," Dathan pointed to the black stone lying on a red velvet cushion. "And the many colored jasper of Benjamin's. See, as the light strikes it, it is red; now, as I turn it in my hand, it is green. See, look, it even turns black."

"Why should Aaron be given all these stones?" Abiram whispered angrily.

"And why should he be priest? Why should he lord it over us?" Dathan asked in turn.

"Come, let's waste no more time. What are we here for?" Abiram began to open his chamois bag and reached out to pick up the jasper and the pearl. But, just as his fingers were closing over the jasper, the front flap of the tent opened, and one of the soldiers called in, "Who goes there?"

Dathan and Abiram froze, motionless. They held their breath, standing stiffly, and the guard, his eyes not accustomed to the gloom, did not see them. Over his shoulder he said to his companions, "It must have been the wind."

"No, it sounded to me like men whispering," the other guard said. "I'll bring a torch. We'll go in and make sure there is no one there."

He closed the flap, and Dathan and Abiram released their breath. That was a close call. Once more Abiram reached out for the precious stones, but Dathan held his arm. He stepped close to Abiram and breathed softly into his ear.

"Fool! The guards will return. Hurry! We must leave!"

Quietly, on tiptoe, hardly disturbing the air, the two moved softly and swiftly through the tent, squirmed under the canvas, and escaped empty-handed into the shadows.

They moved on for several yards before they dared talk. Then Dathan stopped and grasped Abiram's arm.

"Look, we are near Korah's tent. Let's wake him up. We can make new plans with him."

They moved forward quietly. At the entrance to Korah's tent, they called his name softly, not to disturb his wife or sons. They wanted no one but Korah in on their secret.

He heard their whisper because he was not asleep. He was lying on his bed, scheming of ways to become High Priest in place of Aaron. So, when they called him, he heard and slipped out of bed. Without disturbing anyone, he threw a cloak over his shoulders and moved cautiously outside. When he saw Dathan and Abiram, he motioned them to follow and crept away with them to the other side of the camp where they could talk without being overheard.

As soon as they were seated on the ground and had caught their breath, Dathan and Abiram told Korah what they had tried to do that evening.

When he heard their story, Korah exclaimed, "Fools! You would have ruined everything! Stealing the gems would not keep Aaron from becoming High Priest. No, we must go to Moses and demand fair play. Let me handle this. I shall go to him and openly challenge his appointment of Aaron."

Not caring that it was nighttime and that Moses would be asleep, Korah, Abiram, and Dathan went openly and boldly to the tent of Moses and summoned him out. Moses came to the door and said quietly, "Is there an enemy in the camp that you summon me from my sleep?"

"No," Korah answered curtly.

"Is there rebellion then?" Moses asked.

At first the three men did not answer. Then Korah, with an impatient movement of his hand, said, "Very well, Moses, there is rebellion. We come to oppose your appointment of Aaron as High Priest."

Moses smiled. "Who is your candidate?"

Korah stepped back and stared at Moses. "Why, myself, of course! Was I not Pharaoh's treasurer? Am I not important? Everyone considers me great but you, Moses. You have been very unfair to me. You should have appointed me chief of the Kehoth division of the Levites. Instead you chose my cousin, Elizaphan. Make up for this mistake. Appoint me now as High Priest of Israel!"

Moses smiled again. "I thought perhaps you were going to object because *I* had not been made High Priest. Indeed, when God made the choice, I confess I was surprised that my brother Aaron was chosen instead of me."

Dathan interrupted him rudely. "When God chose! That is what you say! But I say that you yourself decided on this appointment. God had nothing to do with it!"

"Slowly, slowly, Dathan," Moses said, no longer smiling. "You say to my face that I lie?"

Abiram stepped forward and said insolently, "Yes, I say it. This time you did not receive any command from God. Aaron is your brother. You wanted to give more honor to your own family."

Now Moses smiled again. Then, surprised by a sound behind him, he turned and saw that their voices had disturbed the sleep of many people, and one by one from the tents in the desert they came and stood about, listening to this argument. Moses turned back to the three men.

"You rebel against my brother and me because you think we are greedy for more power," he said. Then proudly, "The honor of my family is high enough. I had no need to raise it higher. God commanded that Aaron become the High Priest."

"And it is what we wish!" someone called from the crowd.

"Yes, yes," shouted another. "Aaron has given us the blessing of peace. Aaron shall be our High Priest. No one but Aaron!"

"You see," Moses said to Korah, Dathan, and Abiram. "God wants Aaron, I want him, and the people want him. How can you object?"

"Oh," Korah said scornfully, "the people. You have always influenced the people as you wished. They will say anything you want them to say. But, that it is God's command . . . no, you cannot make me believe that."

Now Moses spoke angrily. "No, I cannot make you believe it, and I don't care whether you believe it or not. But I shall prove it to the people. As for you three, you tire me with your scheming. I am weary of your constant rebellions. Guards!" he ordered.

Six guards stepped forward.

"Seize these men," Moses commanded.

Before Korah, Dathan, or Abiram could protest, and they didn't even try because all the people were muttering at them, they were seized by the six guards who grasped them firmly by the arms.

"Take them to the Prison Tent," Moses ordered. "Guard them well. They shall be dealt with later."

Everyone watched the guards march the prisoners away. Then Moses turned to the people and said quietly, "Now you will see the proof."

"We don't need any proof, Moses," someone in the crowd called out.

"But proof you shall have," he said sternly. "I shall show you." He turned to all the people gathered in the night which was beginning to draw to a close. "God hopes that someday all of Israel shall become a holy people and a kingdom of priests. Until that time shall come, Aaron shall be the symbol of our holiness. Aaron shall be the sign of a priestly people. Now listen to me. I have declared the command of God, that I appoint Aaron as the High Priest of Israel. And now, so that all may know that it is the truth, I shall give you proof from God."

He turned to Eldad and Medad, two of the wise men who had come to his side during this argument.

"Eldad," Moses said, "bring me a beam of wood. Medad, bring me an ax."

Both men hurried away. Everyone waited patiently until Eldad came hurrying back to Moses, a beam of wood hoisted on his shoulder, and Medad came running at his side with a hatchet in his hand. Now all eyes turned to Moses.

Moses placed the beam of wood on the ground, raised the hatchet, bringing it down eleven times. With eleven blows he chopped the wood into twelve even pieces. Then, as he handled these pieces of wood, they grew thin and long and round. Suddenly they turned into rods.

"Now," he commanded, "the leader of each of the twelve tribes, step forward."

Up stepped Nahshon, the head of the tribe of Judah. To him Moses handed a quill.

"Take this quill-pen," Moses said, "and write your name on this rod, then the name of your tribe."

And Nahshon wrote: "Nahshon of the tribe of Judah." He returned the rod to Eldad and stepped back. Up stepped Nethanel. He wrote on the rod which Moses handed him: "Nethanel of the tribe of Reuben." Then he, too, handed his rod to Medad. Then up stepped Eliah, and on his rod he wrote: "Eliah of the tribe of Zebulun."

One by one the chiefs of eleven of the tribes wrote their names and the names of their tribes on each of the eleven rods. Then up stepped Aaron, and Moses handed him the last rod.

"Aaron, write your name and the name of your tribe on this twelfth rod."

And Aaron wrote: "Aaron of the tribe of Levi." He handed the quill to Moses and the rod to Eldad.

Moses turned again to face the people. "Now," he said, "come with me to the sanctuary."

Moses started forward, Eldad on one side carrying six of the rods, Medad on the other side carrying the other six rods, Aaron behind them, followed by all the people. When they reached the sanctuary, Moses halted the procession.

"You yourselves have seen the beam of wood from which I chopped out these rods. You yourselves have seen the heads of each of the twelve tribes write their names and the names of their tribes on these rods. You yourselves now see that I have not touched these rods, nor has there been anything else added to them. Is that not true?"

"Yes, yes," the people called out.

Moses turned to Eldad and Medad.

"Yes, yes," they said.

To Aaron, Moses asked, "And what do you say?"

"Yes, it is as you say," Aaron answered.

"Very well then." Moses motioned to Eldad and Medad. "These rods will be placed in the sanctuary until the eighth hour. Now the hour stands at four in the morning. We shall wait here, all of us, to see that no person goes into the tabernacle to touch the rods while they lie on the altar. At the eighth hour we shall examine them for the proof which God will send us."

Eldad and Medad went into the sanctuary alone. On the altar they spread out the twelve rods in a row. Then they came out and sat down with Moses to wait for the eighth hour.

It was a long wait, but no one changed positions. Some people fell asleep. Someone yawned and wondered aloud why they needed this proof. Others whispered among themselves, wondering about the punishment which Korah, Dathan, and Abiram would be given for trying to incite this rebellion. Others just waited, as the hours passed, slowly, one after the other.

Finally the hours wore away. Now it was the eighth hour of the morning.

Moses stood up, and suddenly everyone was wide awake. There was no yawning, no rubbing of eyes. There was no mumbling, no stretching of muscles. Everyone stood up to see what Moses had to show them.

"Now," he said, "we shall all go into the sanctuary together."

Eldad and Medad allowed Moses and Aaron to precede them, then followed, and the people were close on their heels. Moses walked directly to the altar where the twelve rods had been placed.

Picking up the first one on which was written: "Nahshon of the tribe of Judah," Moses said, "You see, this rod remains as it was when Nahshon inscribed it." And he picked up the second rod. Someone called out impatiently, "We see, Moses, we see!"

"The rod of Aaron!" shouted another. "Show us the rod of Aaron!"

Everyone could see that all eleven rods were exactly as they had been when placed on the altar. But something marvelous had happened to the rod with the name of Aaron of the tribe of Levi!

On the rod of Aaron there leaped out in blazing letters the name of God! From all over the wood, blossoms of the almond tree sprouted, and with the flowers were the fruit, the ripe almonds.

Moses picked up this wonderful rod with its ripened fruit and blossoming flowers, glowing with the Divine Name, and held it up for all the people to see.

"Here is the evidence of God's wish," he said. "God has caused the rod of Aaron to bear God's name and to blossom. Aaron is the priest of Israel. Aaron is the High Priest of all the children of Israel."

And the people called out, "Aaron is the priest! Aaron is the High Priest of the children of Israel."

Moses handed Aaron the Rod of Almonds. Aaron, holding it high for all to see, in a voice clear and steady, recited, "May God bless you and keep you."

Commentary

The next day Moses entered the Tent of the Pact, and there the staff of Aaron of the house of Levi had sprouted: it had brought forth sprouts, produced blossoms, and borne almonds.

Numbers 17:23

* * *

The role of Aaron in the biblical account of the Exodus is in many ways a mysterious one. Throughout most of the major events, Aaron plays a central role, standing beside his brother Moses and speaking for Moses on many occasions. It is his staff that turns into a serpent in Pharaoh's court. Later it is his rod that is held over the rivers that turn to blood during the plagues. (Exod. 7:20) Sometimes it even seems that Moses and Aaron combined make one complete man. Yet, at the same time, Aaron remains largely in the background, his biblical portrait not nearly as detailed as that of Moses.

After all he had contributed, it would seem self-evident that Aaron should have the right to serve as the first High Priest of Israel. Yet the Torah reports widespread resistance to this appointment; other tribes wanted this great honor for themselves. The matter was resolved when God directed Moses to take a staff from each of the chieftains of the twelve tribes, inscribe the name of the tribe on each, and leave them in the Tent of the Pact, with the understanding that the staff that blossomed would belong to the tribe selected to initiate the priestly line. (Num. 17:16–20) This is done, and it is the staff of Aaron— the very staff involved in so many prior miracles—that blossoms. Thus is the matter settled.

*   *   *

The miracle of the blossoming rod is echoed in the midrashic account of the boy Abraham, who is catapulted inside a furnace by Nimrod. Miraculously, the wood piled for the fire instead blossoms and bears fruit. (See "The Garden in the Fire" and the accompanying commentary in the first volume of *Bible Legends: An Introduction to Midrash*.) Those steeped in Torah would recognize the biblical echo of this miracle. This very detail links Abraham not only to Aaron but, of course, to Moses, who carries out the test for God.

*   *   *

Why, we might ask, does God so often resort to the use of miracles to resolve a dispute or to save those in peril? In some instances, there may be no other way of rescuing people, as at the Reed Sea. In other instances, miracles remind the people of God's presence in determining their destiny, as in this case of the blossoming staff of Aaron. Miracles, of course, commonly are found in all mythology, legend, and folklore. Can you think of a fairy tale in which no single miracle or act of magic occurs? Probably not. One of the essential purposes of the Hebrew Bible is to serve as the body of myths, legends, and folklore of our people, and therefore it is natural for miracles to play a central role in these accounts.

Write Your Own Midrash

Write a midrash that uses a familiar miracle in a different setting. Most miracles can be transplanted to a different context although certain events, such as the parting of the Reed Sea, seem uniquely linked to their original biblical context. But such miracles as the blossoming staff, the falling manna, or the water that pours forth from a rock could be used to animate other situations as well. Still, it is worth noting and appreciating how perfectly each biblical miracle fits into its particular context.

❧ 10 ❧

Og and the Ants

As the Israelites approached the Promised Land, Moses sent scouts to report on those already inhabiting it. The scouts returned with the news that "giants" lived there. Eventually the Israelites conquered this enemy. Among those conquered was Og, the king of Bashan. Although there are only few biblical references to Og, in Jewish legend he became identified as a giant whose defeat was a miracle for Israel. And who defeated this giant? Some of the smallest creatures in the world—the ants.

I
t was twilight, and the night was coming on quickly. Moses ordered a halt at the outskirts of Edrei. The people could go no further tonight. They were tired. They had just defeated Sihon, the powerful king of the Amorites, in a fierce battle. They wanted to be done with fighting; they wanted to rest.

"We're safe enough here," they said to Moses. "Let's pitch our tents here on the outskirts of Edrei and make camp."

After a brief council with the leaders, Moses agreed that here at Edrei they were safe. He sent out the order to make camp, and everyone sighed in relief.

But, just as the order was given, one of Moses' spies came

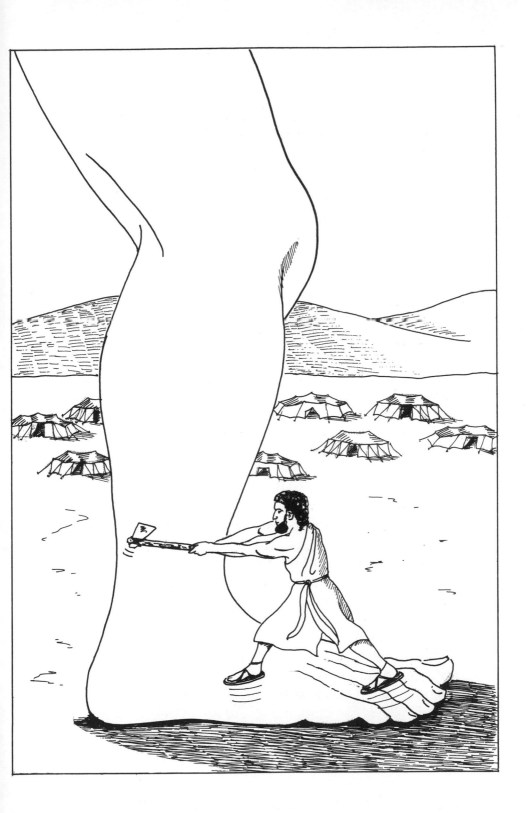

running to him from the city of Edrei where he had been sent
to scout out the land. He was breathless and frightened. His
eyes rolled wildly, and he could hardly talk. But finally he man-
aged to gasp, "Flee, Moses, flee! We are in the greatest danger!
We are doomed!"

Moses took hold of his arm and shook him a little to quiet
him so he could speak more clearly.

"It's the giant, Og," he cried. "He rules over Edrei. He is
bigger even than the three giants of Canaan. He will crush us
all with one stamp of his boot! Flee, Moses, flee!"

Alarm swept through the people.

"More danger!"

"Are we never to be safe?"

"Where shall we run now?"

But Moses smiled; then he laughed out loud! When the people
heard him laugh, they thought, "If our wise leader laughs in
the face of this danger, then evidently the danger cannot be so
great." So they stopped their own chattering and listened to
Moses.

"Who is Og," he said, mockingly, "that you should fear him?
We have defeated the Edomites and Amalek. In the Valley of
Arnon we were successful in battle, and we smashed the armies
of Sihon and his Amorites. Balak, the king of Moab, and Balaam
we crushed. God fights on our side, and we are always the
victors. And do you then really fear one giant whose name is
Og?"

Moses was teasing the people, and they laughed. Then, realizing how victorious they had indeed been against all these great
armies, they felt proud and confident once more.

Loud murmurs of agreement rose. The people shouted, re-
minding each other of their conquests.

"Remember the Valley of Arnon," someone shouted. "Were
we trapped in the valley between the two mountains by the
Amorites? No! God moved the rocky mountain into the pointed

mountain, and the Amorites were crushed, and we were safe. Why be afraid of Og, the giant?"

"That's right!" cried another. "Remember Heshbon? We could have been killed there by King Sihon's soldiers, but God drew masks over their faces, and they killed each other instead of us! So why be afraid of Og, the giant?"

"Who's afraid of the big, great Og?"

"Who's afraid of the big, great Og?"

All the people picked up this refrain and began singing, "Who's afraid of the big, great Og?" They repeated the phrase over and over, laughing and singing, and the children took it up and chanted it over and over. And so they went to bed, all of them, singing, "Who's afraid of the big, great Og?"

Soon all the camp was dark and quiet. Only the sentries walked their posts. All else was still. The people slept.

Only Moses did not sleep. He sat at the door of his tent, staring into the black night. In his ears he could still hear the singing, "Who's afraid of the big, great Og?"

Well, *he* was afraid. Moses was very much afraid of Og. He knew how big and how powerful this giant was. He was so big, so huge, that his thigh bone alone was twelve miles long! He was twenty-four miles tall! Twenty-four miles!

Moses shifted on the cold ground, remembering the stories he had heard about this giant. Never in his life could Og sleep on a wooden bed or sit on a wooden chair. They broke like toothpicks! His beds and his chairs were made of the strongest iron!

Moses closed his eyes and remembered more. In one day Og ate one thousand oxen and drank one thousand quarts of water. Oh, Moses was afraid, and not only because of the giant. In spite of what he had told the people, perhaps this time God would not be on their side. Perhaps in the war they had just fought with Sihon, king of the Amorites, they had committed sins. God would not help those who were sinful.

So all through the night, Moses sat at the door of his tent, staring into the night, brooding and worrying, while the people slept soundly. Hadn't Moses told them not to be afraid? So they slept. And Moses sat there, hour after hour. But while he sat and worried, he also prayed.

Before the dawn broke, Moses felt stronger again, full of courage. He decided on a quick attack upon the city of Edrei and on Og, the giant. Just at dawn, while the light was still gray, Moses awakened the people and prepared to attack the city. But, as he turned back to Edrei, he looked at the city and cried out in alarm.

"Look! They have built a new wall around the city!"

But it was not a new wall. What Moses could not see at first in the dim light of the dawn was that this was the giant, Og, sitting on top of the old wall. With his head lost in the clouds and his feet touching the ground, he looked like a high wall.

Then, when the people realized that this was the giant, they turned to run away. The captains and lieutenants had hard work holding them back. It was Moses finally who quieted them.

"Wait! Wait!" he said, shouting above the noise. "Wait, don't run. You won't have to fight. This is going to be a duel between Og and me."

"How can you attack that giant?" someone shouted.

"You'll be killed," someone else yelled.

"Don't go, Moses, don't go!"

"I won't," he said as calmly as he could. "I'll wait for Og to attack me."

Now Og, sitting on top of the wall surrounding his sixty cities, looked at the camp of the Israelites and sneered.

"Why, they're just a puny lot," he said. "I can crush them with one blow. Let's see now," he said, trying to measure the camp with his eyes. "Let's see. That camp is about twelve miles in circumference. Ho! This is going to be simple, as easy as crushing an ant."

He stood up, and the ground shook. With steps at least a mile long, he strode towards the mountains, making the very ground under his feet tremble with every step.

At the mountains, Og put out his giant hand.

"Here is a mountain that is twelve miles wide. I shall tear up this mountain and throw it on Israel's camp, crushing every one of them!"

Pulling at the mountain, without even straining his muscles, he tore it up out of its mooring in the rocks. He placed the mountain on top of his head, without even breathing hard under the strain. Then he turned; step by step he moved in the direction of the camp.

The people cried out. "Save us, Moses. Save us!"

"I shall," Moses said quietly and calmly.

On and on came Og, balancing the huge mountain on his head. The earth shook, and the trees shivered; the stones groaned, and the rivers wept. On and on came Og, step by step. All the animals fled from the advancing giant.

But there was one little army of animals that was not afraid. The ants that crawl on the ground and are so easily crushed— they were not afraid. While Og was stalking the people of Israel with the mountain as his weapon, God whispered to the leader of the ants. The leader understood in a moment what to do, and he sounded the bugle call of the ants, a call that only the ants heard and understood. In a twinkling they began crawling in from everywhere.

"One battalion to the left," the leader called. "One battalion to the right. Two in the center. On your mark, march!"

All the ants from all over the countryside began crawling up the mountain which Og was carrying on his head.

"Attack!" the leader shouted.

The ants burrowed and dug into the mountain, deeper and deeper, harder and faster. They crawled, and they dug, and they chewed away the grains of earth all around the giant's neck. And suddenly—success! The ants had dug a big hole through the mountain around Og's neck. All at once the mountain fell over his head, right onto his shoulders!

Og was trapped!

He pushed at the mountain. He twisted. He squirmed. He threw his huge shoulders from right to left. He shouted. He roared. But he was trapped. He could not budge the mountain.

Then Moses snatched up a big ax that was eighteen feet long and started to run towards Og to finish him off.

"Strike his heart!"

"Strike at his neck!"

But Moses knew the giant's weak spot. If he could only reach high enough up into the air to strike a hard blow to Og's *ankle*, Og would die.

So Moses took a deep breath, gathered all his strength, crouched, and then he sprang! He leaped fifteen feet into the air and struck a heavy blow to Og's ankle with the ax.

The mighty Og let out one loud cry, tottered, staggered, and collapsed on the ground, smothered by the mountain.

Moses and the children of Israel were rescued once more. With the army of ants leading the way, they marched safely into Edrei.

Commentary

Only Og king of Bashan was left of the remaining Rephaim [giants].   Deuteronomy 3:11

*   *   *

This single biblical reference to Og, the king of Bashan, as the last of the remaining Rephaim (understood to mean "giants"), gave birth to a rich tradition. According to this tradition, Og was the only giant to survive the Flood, riding on Noah's ark. Many sightings and stories about him are found both in the Midrash and in Jewish folklore, the earliest portraying him as a fierce enemy of the Jewish people, consistent with the biblical portrayal. But the later legends present him in a more favorable light, as a well-intentioned but still terrifying giant.

* * *

The combat between Moses and the giant Og parallels, of course, the combat between David and Goliath. David defeats Goliath with a child's weapon, the sling; in the case of Og and Moses, Og is defeated by the smallest of opponents, the ants, who burrow through the mountain he intends to use to crush Israel, causing it to collapse upon the giant. Moses then completes the conquest by leaping up and striking a blow to Og's ankle, after which the giant drops to the ground and dies. The moral of this story, like that of David and Goliath, seems clear: Israel, a tiny nation, is able to defeat much greater adversaries because of the support of God and the bravery and unity of its people in the face of adversity. This moral is emphasized by the ants, tiny creatures, who by working together defeated a giant.

* * *

There is another version of the defeat of Og where the defeat comes, not from the ants, but from the name of God. In this alternate legend, Og uproots the mountain, lifts it up in the air, and casts it upon Israel's camp where it would have crushed everyone. But Moses had written the name of God upon a potsherd and had thrown it at the mountain, causing the mountain to remain suspended in the air. (*Midrash Devarim Rabbah* 1:24) This is, of course, a miracle of God, one of many in Jewish lore said to come through the power of God's name, known as the Tetragrammaton.

* * *

A similar legend about God's name is told about King David, who was said to have located the foundation stone which, according to Jewish lore, is the cornerstone of the world. When he lifted it up, all at once the waters of the abyss started to rise. They would have inundated the world, except that David wrote God's name on a potsherd and threw it into the abyss, causing the waters to recede at once. This legend about King David is found in the Talmud (*Sukah* 53a–b) and was probably the legend that inspired the one about Moses and Og and the mountain. This is typical of the way that one legend gives birth to another, in turn inspiring other legends until, over the ages, a folk tradition as rich as the Jewish one has come into being.

* * *

When the rabbis find a good character, such as Og, they are reluctant to drop him. Even though Og was defeated and killed by Moses, the giant's prior history remained a mystery. And so in the rabbinic legends we find a detailed story in which the character of the vicious Og is transformed into that of a well-intentioned giant. Og helped Noah locate the animals for the ark, journeying to the corners of the world to corral them. When the great Flood came, Og begged Noah to take him along. This created a dilemma for Noah: Og had helped him, but there was no room in the ark for such a giant. When Noah told this to Og, Og suggested that he sit on the roof of the ark. Although worried that the weight of the giant might sink the vessel, Noah, nevertheless, let him sit there. When it did not sink, Noah knew that God intended him to save the giant as well. (*Pirke de-Rabbi Eliezer* 23)

* * *

Although the Midrash does not include stories about Og after he was killed by Moses, stories about the giant can be found in later Jewish folklore. Og became a popular figure in Moslem folklore as well. Among the Jewish tales about Og, there is the following tale told in Eastern Europe: In his wanderings, the giant Og came to Poland in the winter. Not used to such cold weather, he looked for a tailor and demanded a coat to keep him warm. He asked the terrified tailor how long it would take to make the coat. Seeing the size of the giant, the tailor said it would take about a year. Og got angry and said that, if the coat wasn't ready in a week, he would trample the town into dust. The frightened tailor gathered the townspeople together and told them of the giant's demand. The inhabitants scurried off to neighboring towns and brought back every tailor they could find. An army of tailors then set to work on the giant coat, finishing just in time. Suddenly they heard the giant approach. With nowhere else to hide, they jumped inside the pockets of the coat. Og picked up the coat, put it on, and placed his hands into the pockets to warm them, squeezing all the tailors together. Then, warm for the first time since coming to Poland, he lay down to sleep, and the terrified tailors escaped. But, thereafter, every one of them had a pale face. And that is why tailors have pale faces. (*Israel Folktale Archives, #7249*, collected by Samuel Zanvel Pipe from his family)

Write Your Own Midrash

Make up a story about the giant Og set sometime in the past. It could be a fairy tale with a giant, like Jack and the Beanstalk, but it should include some Jewish elements. You may want to add details to the stories about Og and Noah or Og and Moses, or you could compose a completely original story. What would happen if Og showed up in your town or city? Would he be welcomed? Would the army attack or recruit him? Whose side would he be on?

✛ 11 ✛

The Wandering Well

After escaping Pharaoh at the Sea of Reeds, the Israelites wandered for many years through the wilderness. They suffered from hunger and thirst and often regretted having left their homes in Egypt. To ease the burden of their wanderings, God provided guidance and sustenance: an enchanted food called manna fell from heaven to sustain them, a cloud led them during the day, and a pillar of fire led them at night. But where in that vast desert did they find enough water during their long journey? To answer this question, the rabbis created the legend of Miriam's well.

Miriam stood with Moses and Aaron at Kadesh-barnea before the well that had gone dry. Around them crowded the people. She looked at them and was sorry for them. They had gone through much suffering in their escape from Egypt. And now the worst curse of the desert threatened. There was no water.

Moses turned to the Israelites and said, "My people, do not weep. Do not worry. When you were slaves in Egypt, God rescued you. And now you are marching toward the Promised Land."

"But it is so very far," someone muttered.

"It is far," Moses admitted. "But think for a moment. Do you really believe that you have been rescued from Egypt only to perish in the desert?"

He smiled, and Aaron and Miriam smiled with him.

"No," Moses went on, "no, my brothers and sisters, have no fear. God will rescue you again and again as you march through the wilderness."

"But our babies are so thirsty!" a woman cried.

"They will not thirst for long," Moses said calmly. "God is performing a miracle to keep you from thirsting in the desert. Miriam, come here."

Miriam, tall and proud, walked slowly to her brother, her black hair lifted lightly by the wind, her white robe swaying around her ankles. As she reached Moses, she smiled at him, then turned to smile at the people.

"When we came safely out of the Red Sea," she said, "we sang for joy. We were delivered from Pharaoh, and we sang, 'God is my strength and song, and God is my salvation.' Listen now to my brother Moses. He brings you good news."

"Yes, I bring you good news," Moses repeated. "For a long time Miriam has been a prophet, and, because of her goodness and because of her unselfishness, God will perform a miracle through Miriam, a miracle for your benefit. Come, Miriam. Come, Aaron. Come, all."

He and Miriam and Aaron turned and walked to the foot of one of the mountains. The people followed at a distance. Soon they came to a large rock. It was shaped like a sieve.

Moses turned to Miriam. He handed her his rod.

"Take my Sapphire Rod, my sister. Touch the rock."

As Miriam took hold of the rod and lifted her arm, the elders of the twelve tribes cried out, "Spring up, O Well, and sing to your people."

Miriam touched the rock. Water gushed forth. It shot like a geyser into the air, sprinkling those closest to it, then tapered off into an overflowing well of clear water. The rock, which had now become a well, moved a few feet towards Miriam. She backed away, and the well followed her.

"Wherever we go in the desert," Moses said, "this well shall go with us. However long we shall be in the desert, so shall the well. Miriam's well remains with you as long as Miriam shall remain alive!"

"Long live Miriam!"

"Live, Miriam, and help keep us alive!"

The people shouted their relief and their hopes. Miriam had always been a favorite. Now they were grateful and loved her all the more.

All were now happy, but Miriam was happiest of all. Because of her goodness, this well had been given to the people. So she guarded it. She saw that it was kept clean, that no stones were thrown into it, that twigs did not fall into it, and thus the water remained sweet to drink.

Once more, with Moses leading them, the people of Israel took up their wanderings. No more did they fear the desert threat of thirst. Wherever they went, the well followed them. It trudged with them down into deep valleys. It climbed with them up to the tops of mountains. It crawled with them through the rocks and across the stones of the desert. It followed them through the shifting sands.

For the forty years during which the people marched, the well accompanied them. It was there when hunger came upon the people. It saw the manna rain down from heaven. It was there when Moses went to Mount Sinai to receive the Law. It saw the disgrace of the people in building the Golden Calf. Miriam wept at their sin, and the well wept with her. Moses returned and destroyed the Golden Calf, and Miriam rejoiced. And the waters laughed.

And so, as they marched, the well never failed. It was always full to the brim, through the long, cold nights, through the hot, dusty days. A child could carelessly dash some water to the ground, or a grownup could let a cup slip and spill the water. No one scolded; no one complained because the well was always full.

Through all the wars, the well followed. It was there when the Israelites defeated Sihon, the king of the Amorites, and at the battles with Amalek. It watched Moses destroy the giant Og, and as he punished the Edomites. Then, finally, the long, weary years of wandering came to an end. They reached their goal. They stood on the banks of the Jordan!

The people looked across the river and marveled at the beautiful land which awaited them. The well looked too and saw the Promised Land towards which Moses had been leading them.

There was great rejoicing among the people. They bathed themselves in the river and changed into their cleanest garments. They spoke to their children and reminded them of all the wonders which God had worked for them and hoped they were worthy enough to cross the Jordan. They prayed that their life in the Promised Land would be a good life.

The people rejoiced.

But, silently and by itself, the well shed bitter tears. For many days it wept, remembering something everyone else had by now forgotten. It remembered that Moses had said that the well would remain with the children of Israel throughout Miriam's lifetime.

Now forty years had passed since the wandering well had been created because of Miriam's goodness. And in those forty years she had become an old woman. The well knew, though the people did not, that the time of Miriam's death was coming close.

When she would die, the well would dry up and be no more. And so the well, by itself, silently wept.

As the people rejoiced on the banks of the Jordan, Miriam lay in her tent. She was sick and knew that her life was coming to an end. But she did not want to spoil the joy and the pleasure of the people, so she suffered by herself, quietly, waiting for the angel to come and take her soul.

The nighttime came on suddenly, as it did in the desert. The stars were shining, twinkling in the darkness of the night. The moon looked down on earth and saw that everyone in the camp was asleep, everyone except Miriam.

She was awake. Through the open flap of her tent she was looking up into the dark night, and she listened. She thought she heard music. Yes, it was music, beautiful heavenly music, coming closer and clearer. Then an angel drifted down to take her soul.

As the angel began its swift climb upwards through the sky, the music became softer and fainter—and drifted away.

The only thing awake in the desert was the well. It watched the angel going heavenward with the soul of Miriam. And it began to weep and, as it wept, its tears, flowing faster and faster, took all the waters out of its depth.

The well began slowly to dry up. All through the long hours of the night the well gave up more and more of its waters, drying up and drying up. By the time the first clear rays of the sunlight broke through the veil of the dim dawn, the well was completely dry. It had wept itself away.

So, on the banks of the Jordan River, where there was water aplenty, the wandering well, which God gave to the people of Israel as an honor to Miriam, gave forth its last little drop of water.

It became once more what once it was, a hard and solid rock.

Commentary

[That] *is the well where the Lord said to Moses, "Assemble the people that I may give them water."* Numbers 21:16

* * *

After the Exodus from Egypt, the children of Israel wandered in the wilderness for forty years. Where did they find enough water to drink? The Bible tells us that God told Moses to gather the people together so that they could drink from a well. This passage gave birth to many beautiful legends about the well. Just as manna fell from heaven to provide the Israelites with food in the desert, Miriam's well, named after the sister of Moses, followed them wherever they went.

* * *

Why were the Israelites blessed with such a wonderful well? Because God cared for them, and this was one way that God demonstrated love for the people of Israel. God also provided the pillar of cloud by day and the pillar of fire at night to lead them on the way. (Exod. 13:21–22) But there was also another reason for the well—Miriam. The Bible tells us that she, like Moses, was a great prophet. The Talmud states that the well was really following Miriam because of her merits. (*Ta'anit* 9a) That is why it became known as Miriam's well.

* * *

The well also plays an important role in another biblical story. It was at a well that Eliezer, the servant of Abraham, sought and found a wife for Isaac. Throughout the ages a freshwater well has always been considered a great blessing, for life cannot be sustained without water. Thus the well became a symbol for that which provides and sustains life.

* * *

For the Jewish people the Torah is like a well. It is always fresh and vital, guiding and sustaining us as a people. And, like Miriam's well, it comes with us wherever we go. The Bible itself does not say that the well at which the Israelites drank accompanied them in their wanderings. After the well is mentioned, the next passages merely list the places through which the Israelites journeyed. But, for the rabbis, the fact that one passage followed another in the Torah suggested that the two were linked. Therefore, the rabbis assumed that the places listed were not only those where the Israelites camped but also where Miriam's well came to a rest for the people to drink from it.

* * *

According to the Talmud, Miriam's well was one of the ten things created on the eve of the Sabbath at twilight during the days of the Creation. (*Pesachim* 54a) Since this means that the well existed long before the time of the Exodus, other rabbinic legends suggest that it not only followed the Israelites in that time but that, "every place where our forefathers went, the well preceded them." (*Pirke de-Rabbi Eliezer* 35)

* * *

In our story the well is described as drying up at the time of Miriam's death. In another version of the legend, Miriam's well reaches the Holy Land along with the Israelites and is hidden in the Sea of Galilee. (*Shabbat* 35a) A Yiddish legend describes the well as having found its final resting place in the Garden of Eden. (*Ma'aseh me-ha-Hayyat*, Vilna:1908) This story, "Miriam's Tambourine," can be found in the book *Miriam's Tambourine*, edited by Howard Schwartz, pp. 1–7.

Write Your Own Midrash

What do you think happened to Miriam's well after her death? Write a midrash about someone who discovers Miriam's well while on some voyage or journey. Are the waters of the well still fresh? What purpose do they serve now?

⚜ 12 ⚜

The Kiss of God

The accomplishments of Moses are overwhelming. Not only did Moses free the Israelites from Egyptian slavery and receive the Torah, but he guided the people through the wilderness to the Land of Israel. Yet Moses was not permitted to enter the land of his dreams. Why not? Because he disobeyed God at one point, refusing to speak to a rock as commanded and striking it with his staff instead. Moses' life ended while his people were still in the wilderness, but, because of his long devotion to both God and his people, death came to him by the kiss of God.

Moses stood on the summit of Mount Abarim. He gazed upon the scene spread out below him. He saw the road leading up to the mountain gleaming like wet marble. And out of the crystal-like, clear air came the voice of God.

The moment was a great one, great in its tragedy for Moses. God and he were engaged in an argument, and Moses was losing. God spoke gently but firmly, bringing a message solemn and sad.

"My children shall cross the Jordan, all but you, Moses. The time for your death has come!"

Moses thought his heart would break. He began to plead.

"But, God of the universe, my grief is too great to bear! What wrong have I done that You should punish me so? To Your service I gave my whole life. Forty years I struggled in the wilderness, for Your sake. When the children of Israel were stubborn and difficult, I was patient. When our enemies warred against us, I fought them back step by step. O God, now I must hear You decree that I may not enter the Promised Land!"

"You shall not cross the Jordan, Moses," God said.

"But they will need me there. It is a land of idolatry. When they came out of idol-worshiping Egypt, it was I who brought them to a knowledge of Your Law. I persuaded them to live by Your teachings. Now they may march on into Canaan, and I, Your servant, may not enter."

"No, Moses," God said, "you cannot enter. Here in the desert you will die. You will not live to enter the Promised Land."

"O God of the universe," Moses pleaded, "why do You punish me? Why must I die? Why, O God, why?"

The white air around the summit of the mountain was still for a moment. No breeze disturbed it. Then out came God's voice speaking gently.

"Moses, Moses, My faithful Moses. This disappointment comes to every life. No life can have its complete fulfillment. You hope, you dream of many achievements, but no person can live long enough to fulfill every ambition. At the end of every life there still remain all the dreams and hopes that are in the Promised Land. You, My faithful servant, have been fortunate. You have had many rich and rewarding accomplishments. But, even you must leave the earth without realizing every dream, without entering the Promised Land of your hopes."

Gently Moses wept and continued to plead. He had no ambition to *live* in the Promised Land. He wanted only to see for himself that the people would truly arrive in the Promised Land of milk and honey. That was all. Then he would be content to die.

But God said, "Once I admitted you into the Promised Land, you would plead to see the people settled, then to see them build their new homes and till the soil and plant their vineyards. You would want to help them build their schools and raise the sanctuary. No, no, My servant. There would be no end to what you would wish once you were in the Promised Land."

"Not for myself alone," Moses pleaded. "I wish to live for You, to teach Your laws."

"Moses, Moses," God said gently. "Look at nature. See the flower. It is born in the springtime. It lives during a long and pleasant summer. In winter it must die. When first I created the world, I decreed that everything that is born in the world must die, everything, except My people Israel which shall live forever!"

"And I with them!" Moses pleaded.

"Moses, Moses, I ask this question of you. If I would say to you: 'Moses, I have decreed that you must die and the people of Israel shall live forever, but, if you wish, I shall decree that the people of Israel must die, and Moses shall live forever.' Which would you choose, Moses?"

"O Creator of the world, there is no choice!" Moses cried. "The people of Israel shall live forever! There is no choice! I am ready to die!"

Slowly the splendor of the sky dimmed, and Moses felt that now he was alone on the top of the mountain. He sat down and wept. He wept and cried aloud.

"God the Eternal does not change, and Israel lives forever. Yet I do not wish to die but live and declare the works of God!"

Only the gentle winds answered. They caressed him softly, trying to ease his grief.

"Don't be afraid, Moses," said one little zephyr. "It doesn't hurt a bit to die."

"Oh, no," a breeze spoke up. "Why, it's the easiest thing there is."

"An angel comes," said a spurt of wind, "and takes your soul and carries it up into the great, white sky, while the heavenly choir sings beautiful songs, and the cherubim pluck the strings of the silver harp."

While the winds whispered to Moses, God whispered to the angels.

"Gabriel, go now and fetch me the soul of Moses."

But Gabriel answered, "O God, I could not bring death to Your prophet. At Your command he delivered the people of Israel out of the bondage of slavery. I cannot take the soul of this righteous man."

Then God said to Michael, "Michael, go and fetch Me the soul of Moses."

But Michael said, "O God, I could not bring death to Your beloved servant. At Your command he led the people of Israel through the wilderness to the Promised Land. I cannot take the soul of this righteous man."

Before Michael had finished, the angel Samael stamped his foot and said in a loud, angry voice, "O God, am I not the Angel of Death? Why then do You send these others? Isn't it my privilege to bring You the souls of all mortals? Then why not Moses? Is he greater than Adam or Abraham or Isaac? It was I who brought You the souls of these noble ones. Why is Moses different? Give me permission, O God, and I shall fetch his soul."

Samael was poised to wing his way down to the mountain top where Moses wept alone with only the winds for comfort. But God stopped him and said, "You, Samael, how could you take his soul? Would you take it from his face?"

"From his face, O God," Samael said confidently.

"But he once looked upon My face. Then how could you approach his face? Perhaps you mean to take his soul from his hands?"

"From his hands, O God," Samael said, nodding.

"But in his hands My hands placed the Torah. Then how could you approach his hands? Perhaps you plan to take his soul from his feet. But remember, Samael, his feet stood bare by the Burning Bush. How then would you fetch Me the soul of Moses?"

Samael drew himself up tall and said proudly, "I do not know how just yet, O God. But I am the Angel of Death; I know my task. Just give me Your permission."

Then God said, "You have My consent. Go, fetch Me the soul of Moses."

At that moment, the cherubim plucked one chord of the silver harp, and a lonesome note of music echoed through the heavens. The heavenly choir picked up the note and began to hum it softly.

Samael, with the consent of God ringing in his ears, and the heavenly music floating round his head, went away from the Throne of Glory. Getting himself ready for the contest, confidently and proudly, he took his sword in his hand, put on his girdle of cruelty, wrapped himself in his cloak of fury, and in a terrible rage went to find Moses.

By the time Samael reached the mountain top, Moses had stopped weeping. In the light, clear air, in large figures made of fire, he was writing God's name, and there it hung in the sky. Moses no longer looked like a mortal, and his eyes shone like the sun.

Even Samael was stricken with terror at the radiance of the countenance of Moses. He bowed low and could hardly speak even when Moses thundered at him. Samael cowered before him, before the fury of his words, before the flaming anger in his eyes.

"How dare you seize my soul which was given to me by God! You have no power to sit where I sit or to stand where I stand. I will not give you my soul!"

In terror Samael fled back to the Throne of Glory. He had

gone with such joy to get Moses' soul and now he returned, defeated. And God in great anger said to him, "O wicked one! You were created out of fire and to fire you will return. In proud joy you went to bring death to Moses! But, when you saw how great he was, you were frightened. Go, Samael, go down to Moses, go once again, but once again you will return in shame."

This time Samael unsheathed his sword and in a furious temper he shouted, "I shall slay Moses, or he will slay me!"

But, when Samael reached the mountain top, again he was so terrified at the sight of Moses that he fled from him. Moses ran after him, caught him, grappled with him, and brought him to earth. He struck him with his staff, blinded him with the radiance of his face, covered him with shame and confusion. Then, just as Moses was about to slay Samael, a voice from heaven called down.

"Moses, Moses! Do not slay the Angel of Death. The world will always have need of him."

Moses released Samael who bounded away from him, rejoicing at his narrow escape. But Moses, knowing that for him there was no escape, returned to the mountain top to await his end.

When he reached the summit, there stood God and three angels!

The angels, their faces beaming, cried, "Come, Moses, enter into peace."

Then Gabriel arranged Moses' couch. Michael spread over it a purple cover. Zagzagel placed a woolen pillow at the head.

God stood at the head, Michael to God's right, Gabriel to God's left, Zagzagel at the foot. And God said, "Be not afraid. Come, lie down."

Moses stretched out on the couch. And God said, "Cross your feet. Fold your hands upon your breast. Close your eyes. And I will call out your soul with My kiss."

God then kissed Moses, and with this kiss Moses died.

Commentary

So Moses the servant of the Lord died there, in the land of Moab, at the command of the Lord. Deuteronomy 34:5

* * *

Moses, who freed the children of Israel from bondage and brought them the Torah, was not permitted by God to enter the Promised Land. We can imagine the immense frustration of Moses as he was prevented from completing his quest. The traditional reason for God's refusal to let him cross the Jordan is that Moses disobeyed God when he struck the rock in the wilderness for water, rather than speaking to it as God had commanded him to do. Does this seem like a valid reason for such a great punishment? Does the fact that Moses never set foot in the Land of Israel diminish his greatness? The rabbis say that, in a way, it was good that Moses did not complete the quest; otherwise, it would have been difficult to view him as a mortal and not a messianic figure. The rabbis were always vigilant in thwarting any perceived challenge to God's authority. Moses, above all, was a servant of God.

* * *

Even as the rabbis sought to keep Moses from becoming a deity, they felt that such an extraordinary human being could not have had an ordinary death. Also, it is said in the Torah that his body was never found. This gave birth to the legend that Moses died by the kiss of God, or what is called the kiss of the *Shechinah*. In the Talmud *Shechinah* refers to the presence or dwelling of God in this world, but in later Jewish tradition *Shechinah* began to refer to the feminine aspect of God, or to God's bride. Other legends described how the *Shechinah* went into exile with her children, the people of Israel, at the time of the destruction of the Temple. By the later Middle Ages the legends about the *Shechinah* had taken on a life of their own, and she became identified with the Sabbath Queen, who descends to this world every Friday night.

* * *

In addition to the encounter of Moses and the Angel of Death recounted in this story, there are two other famous episodes in Jewish legend. One concerns the talmudic sage Rabbi Joshua ben Levi and the Angel of Death. Rabbi Joshua refused to accompany the angel unless he could hold the angel's sword. Reluctantly, the angel gave it to him, but, when they reached the wall of the Garden of Eden, Rabbi Joshua ben Levi leaped inside and refused to give it back. At last, Rabbi Joshua ben Levi is commanded by heaven to give the sword back to the angel. (*Ketubot* 77b) This parallels the situation in which Moses was about to slay the Angel of Death but was stopped by God. An equally famous talmudic tale concerns King David and the Angel of Death. King David learned from heaven that he was destined to die on a Sabbath. Therefore, he would pray without stopping every Sabbath, knowing that the Angel of Death could not take one who is engaged in prayer. One Sabbath, the angel tricked the king by making a loud noise outside the palace. When King David ran out to see what had happened, the angel grabbed him. (*Shabbat* 30a–b)

Write Your Own Midrash

From the biblical narrative we know that the death of Moses was not an ordinary one and that *no one knows his burial place to this day*. (Deut. 34:6) Write a midrash that describes what happened to Moses when he ascended Mount Nebo. Or write one about how he still lives and about those who encounter him on Mount Sinai or elsewhere. In what situation and where might Moses reappear if he were still alive? There are legends in the Midrash about others who never died and who appear when needed, such as Elijah. Write a midrash about the reentry of Moses into Jewish history.

❧ 13 ❧

Moses Lives Forever

At the end of his life, Moses summoned the Israelites and addressed them at great length; then he climbed Mount Nebo alone. There he viewed the cherished Holy Land that God had promised to Abraham, Isaac, and Jacob, and he took leave of this life. But the life of Moses had been so extraordinary and his communication with God so close and consistent that it was hard to imagine his death to be like that of an ordinary mortal. In fact, his body never was found, *and no one knows his burial place to this day*. (Deut. 34:6) Some say that Moses did not die but lives forever.

The inside of the tent was cool. One strong shaft of light fell on the table at which Joshua sat writing. The parchment on which he wrote was almost completely blank except for the top line. On that line he had written: "God took the soul of Moses with a kiss. And so Moses died."

Joshua drew his eyebrows together in a frown. He was eager to write the whole story but, with all the noise about him, he could scarcely think.

The skies thundered. The seas roared. The earth groaned, and the sun glittered with blazing radiance. The people wept, wildly, unceasingly; they wept and could not be comforted. And

from heaven itself a voice cried out: "Woe! Moses is dead. Woe! Moses is dead!"

Joshua sighed. He too was grieved, but he had to go on with his work. Once more he drew the parchment towards him. As he did, the shaft of light was blotted out by a shadow. Into his tent burst two angry men.

Eleazar and Phineas stood over Joshua and shook their fists in his face.

Eleazar shouted, "Moses is dead! And you sit here writing, as though nothing had happened!"

Phineas cried, "The whole world weeps, the stars, the planets, the sun, and the moon. There never has been a human being like Moses. And yet you sit in your tent and write!"

"And the angels," Eleazar added. "Today in heaven there is no joyous music to be heard as they weep for Moses. And you, Joshua, you sit in your tent and write."

"My friends," said Joshua, "control yourselves. I, too, am heartbroken and, as the new leader, I have just declared a three-month period of mourning."

Eleazar nodded. "Yes, I have heard it announced. For three months the people shall mourn our teacher and leader and friend."

"Well then," Joshua said quietly. "Don't you realize that, after three months have passed, our memories will have faded? We will have forgotten all the small details. It isn't enough to write a history of Moses just by telling how he defeated Pharaoh and led the people through the Red Sea, how he fed them with manna, and how he received the Torah from God and taught it to God's people. It isn't enough just to say that he conquered the wicked kings of other peoples until he led his own people right to the banks of the Jordan. It is my duty now, today, to write down every detail, even of his beautiful death, or we shall forget."

"Yes, yes," agreed Phineas. "Go on."

"We must write down every word which Moses spoke," Joshua

said. "The generations to come will want to know everything we can tell them about our beloved teacher. And so now I write."

"Then remember to say," Eleazar said excitedly, forgetting that he had come to rebuke Joshua, "remember to say that Moses was greater than Adam. Adam was created in God's image but the glory was taken away from him, while Moses retained the radiance which God put in his face forever."

"And be sure to say," Phineas almost interrupted, "that Moses was greater than Noah because, even though Noah saved his own family and the animals in the Flood, Moses saved himself and his whole generation, when they sinned with the making of the Golden Calf."

"Write down these words," Eleazar said, "that he was greater than Abraham because, while Abraham was hospitable, he lived in a land of plenty, while Moses had to feed his people in the barren desert."

"Remember to say why Moses was greater than Isaac . . . ," Phineas said.

"And Jacob . . . ," Eleazar interrupted.

"And Joseph . . . ," Phineas cried out.

Joshua held up his hand. "Please, my good friends, one at a time. Go slowly, please. Each one speak in turn."

Eleazar spoke first. He told how Isaac, led to the altar by Abraham to be sacrificed, beheld the face of the *Shechinah* (the radiance of God). Yet Moses was superior to Isaac. Isaac's eyes grew dim after he had beheld God's face whereas Moses' eyes did not grow dim nor did he lose any of his strength.

Phineas told how Moses was greater than Jacob. Jacob wrestled with an angel and defeated him, but it happened down on earth. But Moses wrestled with angels in heaven when they refused to give up the Torah, and even so he defeated them.

Joshua threw down his quill. "Wait, wait. I am afraid that, after all that we write, the people may still forget Moses. You know it happens even with great ones. People have short memories."

But Eleazar hardly let him finish. "No, no, Joshua. What you say is true. But greater than all mortals was Moses. Oh, no. The people know that they have lost their great teacher, their great leader. No one like Moses will arise again, ever, anywhere in the world."

The three men sat quietly for a moment. Then, before they could break the silence, a messenger came running into the tent, looking for Joshua.

"Joshua," he cried, "come quickly. Come quickly. Jochebed, the aged mother of Moses, searches everywhere for him. She cannot believe he is dead. Please come. She needs your help and consolation."

Joshua ran out of the tent into the streets until he found Jochebed. She would not be comforted; she could not believe that her son Moses was dead. Joshua went with her everywhere to find him.

She went towards Egypt and said, "O Egypt, Egypt, have you seen Moses?"

And Egypt answered, "As truly as you live, Jochebed, I have not seen him since he led the people of Israel out of my land."

Jochebed turned to the Nile and said, "O Nile, O mighty river, have you seen Moses?"

But the Nile replied, "As you live, Jochebed, I have not seen Moses since the day when he turned my waters into blood."

Onward and onward Jochebed went until she came to the Red Sea, and to the Red Sea she cried, "O great sea, O mighty sea, have you seen Moses?"

And the Red Sea answered, "As you live, Jochebed, I have not seen Moses since the day when he cleft my waters in two and marched the people of Israel through the dry land."

Weeping and unconsoled, Jochebed went on and on. When she came to the desert, she said, "O desert, O wilderness, have you seen Moses?"

And the desert replied, "As you live, Jochebed, I have not seen him since the day when he covered me with manna from the heavens."

Then onward she went. And Jochebed went upward to Mount Sinai where she raised her voice and cried, "O Sinai, Sinai, have you seen Moses?"

But Sinai also answered no and said, "As you live, O Jochebed, I have not seen him since the day when he brought the two Tablets of the Law to the children of Israel."

"O Sinai, truly, have you not seen my son?"

Just as Jochebed finished crying these words, there came a gnashing of stones on the shore and a wild gushing of winds. The trees bowed low in the gale, and all the clouds wept with great tears. And from all over the universe there rose one cry from all of nature, from all the people: "O God, have You seen Moses?"

And to their heart came the answer: "Moses lives forever!"

Commentary

No one knows his burial place to this day.　　　Deuteronomy 34:6

✳　✳　✳

The death of Moses was not an ordinary death—he was taken by the kiss of God. (See the previous story and its commentary.) The unusual circumstances of his death, plus the fact that his body was never found, gave birth to the tradition that "Moses lives forever." Here Jochebed, the mother of Moses, goes to all the places where Moses made history—the Nile, the Reed Sea, the desert, and even Mount Sinai—and all of them report that they have not seen Moses since the historic days of old. (*Petirat Mosheh*) This midrash serves a double purpose. First, it acknowledges the universal sense of loss we feel at the death of someone we know, especially a major figure such as Moses. Second, the midrash serves as a reminder that *no one knows his burial place to this day*. (Deut. 34:6) That it is the mother of Moses who is desperately seeking his whereabouts makes the midrash that much more compelling. His mother's loss and grieving are expressed in the words of her search. Finally, there is a hint that, even though Moses had a long and full life, he died prematurely, for there is something wrong when a mother outlives her child.

* * *

The unique circumstances of Moses' death led to the tradition that he entered Paradise alive. In fact, there are various lists in the Talmud of those few who so entered Paradise, including four sages (*Hagigah* 14b), Miriam, and Serah bat Asher. (See the "Introduction" to the first volume of *Bible Legends: An Introduction to Midrash,* pp. xii–xiii, for the legends about Serah bat Asher.) They escaped death in the traditional sense and immediately received their eternal reward for living exemplary lives.

* * *

The lack of concrete evidence of Moses' death, despite the clear statement in the Torah that *Moses the servant of the Lord died there, in the land of Moab, at the command of the Lord* (Deut. 34:5), contributed to the postmidrashic folk tradition that Moses is still alive. This belief is distinctly different from the notion that "Moses lives forever," which implies that Moses, because of all he accomplished, is immortal. People who accomplish a great deal in their lives and are remembered for their accomplishments in future generations are considered to be "immortal," but, of course, that does not mean they are still alive. But the two ideas are sufficiently related that in the folk tradition one easily leads to the other, and that is what happened in this case.

One such folktale of a living Moses was told in Israel by a Moroccan immigrant. In this story a king has a recurring dream in which his aged Jewish slave, Samuel, marries the princess. The king tells the dream to his advisers, who suggest that he send Samuel away on a long quest from which Samuel will never return. They give Samuel a set of riddles and tell him not to come back until he finds Moses, who alone can provide the answers. The slave sets out in despair because he cannot imagine that Moses is still alive. Eventually he comes to the foot of Mount Nebo—the mountain where Moses ascended and disappeared—and falls asleep. When he awakes he discovers a dignified man standing above him. Of course it is Moses, who answers his riddles and some others he has collected on the way which include the secret of a pool that gives eternal youth, the location of a hidden treasure, and the secret of healing leaves that can cure any illness. When Samuel returns to the kingdom as a young, wealthy man, he finds that the princess has become ill, and no doctor can cure her. He seeks an audience, cures her with the healing leaves, and soon becomes her bridegroom, fulfilling the king's prophetic dream. (*Israel Folktale Archives,* #6414, collected by Yaakov Laseri from his father Machlouf Laseri. Also see "The Princess and the Slave" in *Elijah's Violin & Other Jewish Fairy Tales,* edited by Howard Schwartz, pp. 36–43.)

Write Your Own Midrash

Write a tale in which Moses is sought and found alive. Upon such a discovery, what would you (or the characters in your story) say to Moses? How do you think he would feel about the development of the religion to which he devoted his life? Would he be proud that Judaism had survived all this time— some 3,000 years—since the giving of the Torah? What might disappoint him? Cast the story in any form with which you feel comfortable—a midrash, a folktale, or a modern story. Most importantly, portray Moses as a real person, as in the Torah— both proud and humble, single-minded yet not obsessed, and, above all, full of faith in God and the destiny of his people.

Selected Bibliography

ORIGINAL SOURCES IN ENGLISH TRANSLATION

Ben-Amos, Dan, and Mintz, Jerome R., trans. and eds. *In Praise of the Baal Shem Tov (Shivhei Habesht)*. Bloomington: Indiana University Press, 1972.

Braude, William G. *The Midrash on Psalms (Midrash Tehillim)*, 2 vols. New Haven: Yale University Press, 1959.

Charles, R. H., ed. *The Apocrypha and Pseudepigrapha of the Old Testament*, 2 vols. Oxford: Clarendon Press, 1913.

Charlesworth, James H. *The Old Testament Pseudepigrapha*, 2 vols. Garden City: Doubleday, 1983 and 1985.

Danby, Herbert. *The Mishnah*. London: Oxford University Press, 1938.

Epstein, I., ed. *The Babylonian Talmud*. London: Soncino, 1939.

Freedman, H., and Simon, Maurice, eds. *Midrash Rabbah*. London: Soncino, 1939.

Friedlander, Gerald. *Pirke de-Rabbi Eliezer*. New York: Hermon Press, 1970.

Gaster, Moses. *The Chronicles of Jerahmeel* or the *Hebrew Bible Historiale (Sefer Hazichronot)*. New York: Ktav, 1971.

———. *Maaseh Book of Jewish Tales and Legends*, 2 vols. Philadelphia: Jewish Publication Society, 1934.

Glick, S. H., trans. *En Jacob: Aggadah of the Babylonian Talmud*, 5 vols. New York: Hebrew Publishing Co., 1921.

Goldin, Judah, trans. *The Fathers According to Rabbi Nathan (Avot de-Rabbi Nathan)*. New York: Schocken, 1924.

The Holy Scriptures. Philadelphia: Jewish Publication Society, 1955.

131

Noah, Mordecai Manuel, ed. and trans. *The Book of Yashar (Sefer Hayashar)*. New York: Hermon, 1973.

Odeberg, Hugo. *Enoch Three* or the *Hebrew Book of Enoch*. New York: Ktav, 1970.

Sperling, Harry, and Simon, Maurice, eds. *Zohar*, 5 vols. London: Soncino, 1931–34.

The Torah: The Five Books of Moses. Philadelphia: Jewish Publication Society, 1962.

SECONDARY SOURCES

Ausubel, Nathan, ed. *A Treasury of Jewish Folklore*. New York: Crown, 1948.

Barash, Asher, ed. *A Golden Treasury of Jewish Tales*. Tel Aviv: Masada, 1965.

Bialik, Chaim Nachman. *And It Came to Pass: Legends and Stories about King David and King Solomon*. New York: Hebrew Publishing Co., 1938.

Bin Gorion, Micha Joseph, and Bin Gorion, Emanuel, eds. *Mimekor Yisrael: Classical Jewish Folktales*, 3 vols. Bloomington: Indiana University Press, 1976.

Buber, Martin. *The Tales of the Hasidim*. New York: Schocken, 1947–48.

Cohen, A., *Everyman's Talmud*. New York: Schocken, 1975.

Finkelstein, Louis. *Akiba: Scholar, Saint, and Martyr*. Philadelphia: Jewish Publication Society, 1962.

Freehof, Lillian S. *The Bible Legend Book*, 3 vols. New York: Union of American Hebrew Congregations, 1948, 1952, and 1954.

Gaer, Joseph. *The Lore of the Old Testament*. Boston: Little, Brown, 1952.

Gaster, Moses. *The Exempla of the Rabbis*. New York: Ktav, 1968.

Gaster, Theodor, ed. *Myth, Legend and Custom in the Old Testament*. New York: Harper & Row, 1969.

Gersh, Harry. *The Sacred Books of the Jews*. New York: Stein and Day, 1968.

Ginzberg, Louis. *The Legends of the Jews*, 7 vols. Philadelphia: Jewish Publication Society, 1909–35.

Glenn, G. Mendel, ed. *Jewish Tales and Legends*. New York: Hebrew Publishing Co., 1938.

Goldin, Hyman E. *The Book of Legends*, 3 vols. New York: Hebrew Publishing Co., 1938.

Kasher, Menachem M. *Encyclopedia of Biblical Interpretation,* 9 vols. New York: American Biblical Encyclopedia Society, 1980.

Lauderbach, Jacob Z., trans. *Mekilta de-Rabbi Ishmael,* 3 vols. Philadelphia: Jewish Publication Society, 1935.

Nahmad, Hayim Musa, trans. *A Portion in Paradise and Other Jewish Folk Tales.* New York: Norton, 1970.

Noy, Dov. *Folktales of Israel.* Chicago: University of Chicago Press, 1969.

_____. *Moroccan Jewish Folktales.* New York: Herzl, 1966.

Rappoport, A. S. *Myth and Legend of Ancient Israel,* 3 vols. London: Gresham, 1928.

_____. *A Treasury of the Midrash.* New York: Ktav, 1968.

Scholem, Gershom. *Kabbalah.* Jerusalem: Keter, 1974.

_____. *Major Trends in Jewish Mysticism.* New York: Schocken, 1964.

Schwartz, Howard. *Elijah's Violin & Other Jewish Fairy Tales.* New York: Harper & Row, 1983.

_____. *Gates to the New City: A Treasury of Modern Jewish Tales.* New York: Avon Books, 1983.

_____. *Lilith's Cave: Jewish Tales of the Supernatural.* New York: Harper & Row, 1988.

_____. *Miriam's Tambourine: Jewish Folktales from around the World.* New York: The Free Press and Seth Press, 1986. Also, New York: Oxford University Press, 1988.

Spiegel, Shalom. *The Last Trial.* Philadelphia: Jewish Publication Society, 1967.

Urbach, Ephraim E. *The Sages: Their Concepts and Beliefs,* 2 vols. Jerusalem: Magnus Press, 1975.

Vilnay, Zev. *Legends of Jerusalem.* Philadelphia: Jewish Publication Society, 1973.

Wiesel, Eli. *Souls on Fire: Portraits and Legends of Hasidic Masters.* New York: Random House, 1972.